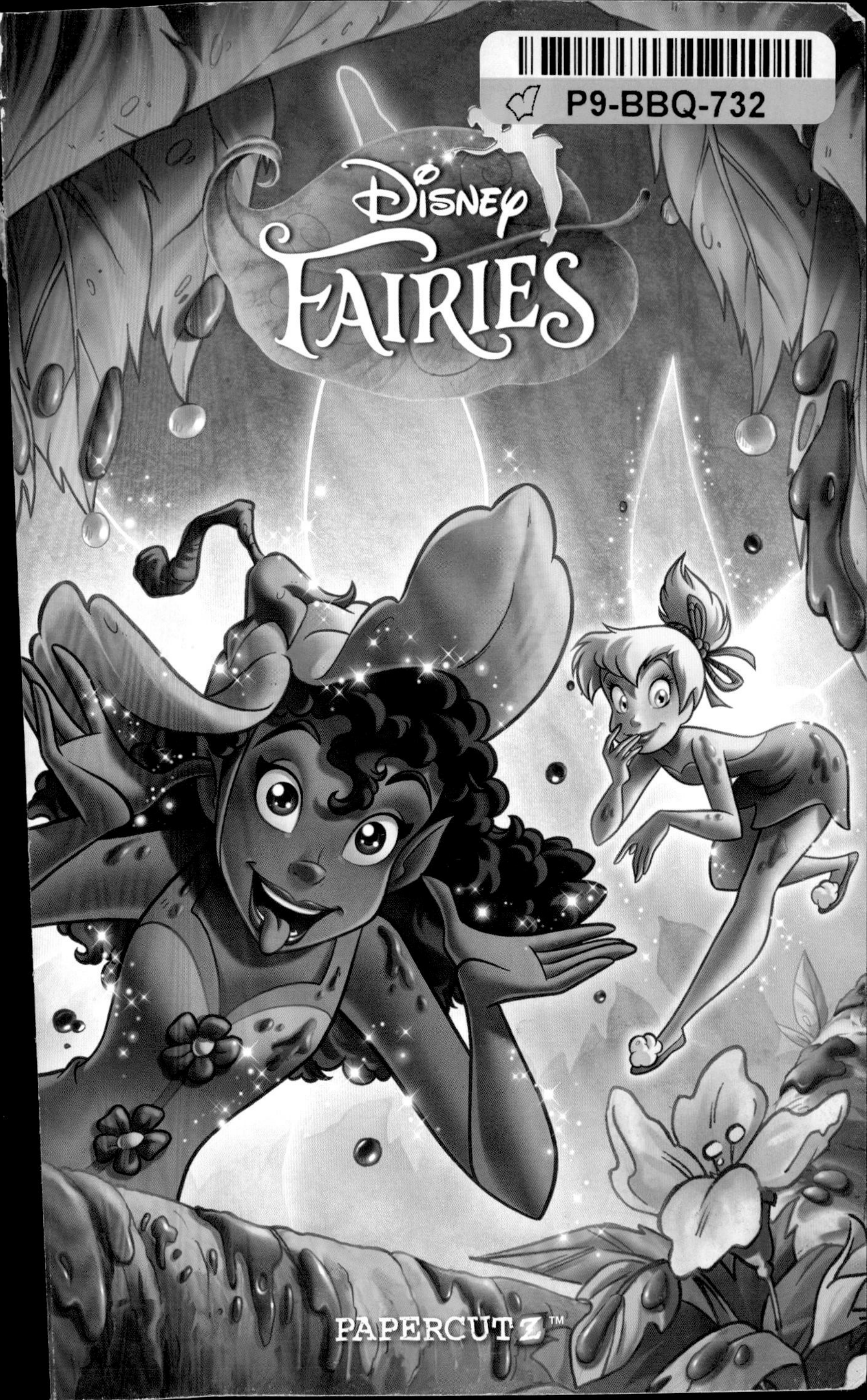
Disney
FAIRIES
PAPERCUTZ™

Graphic Novels Available from PAPERCUTZ

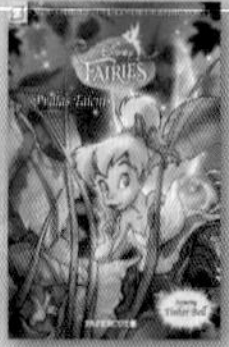

Graphic Novel #1
"Prilla's Talent"

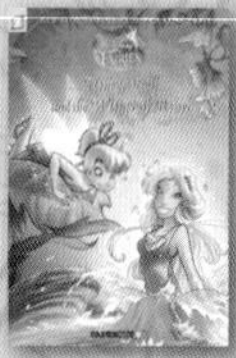

Graphic Novel #2
"Tinker Bell and the Wings of Rani"

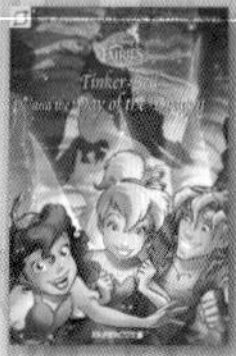

Graphic Novel #3
"Tinker Bell and the Day of the Dragon"

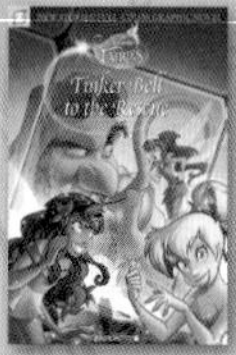

Graphic Novel #4
"Tinker Bell to the Rescue"

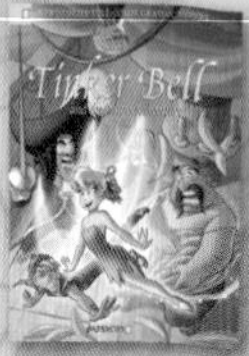

Graphic Novel #5
"Tinker Bell and the Pirate Adventure"

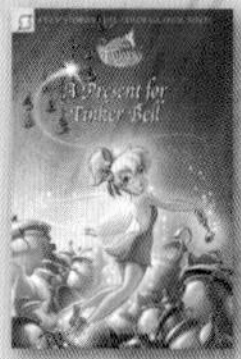

Graphic Novel #6
"A Present for Tinker Bell"

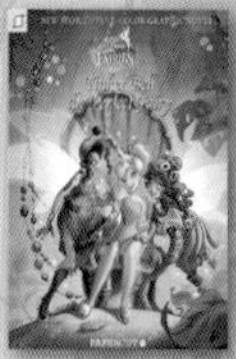

Graphic Novel #7
"Tinker Bell the Perfect Fairy"

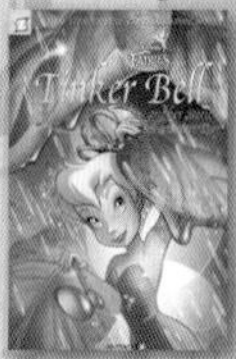

Graphic Novel #8
"Tinker Bell and her Stories for a Rainy Day"

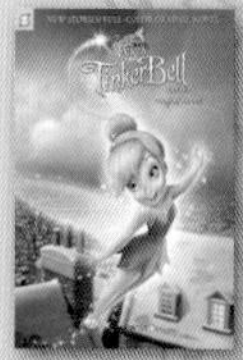

Graphic Novel #9
"Tinker Bell and her Magical Arrival"

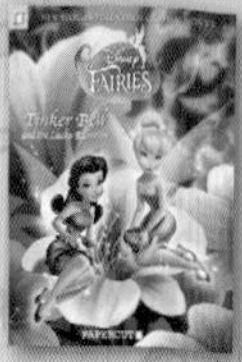

Graphic Novel #10
"Tinker Bell and the Lucky Rainbow"

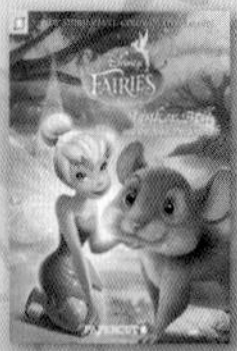

Graphic Novel #11
"Tinker Bell and the Most Precious Gift"

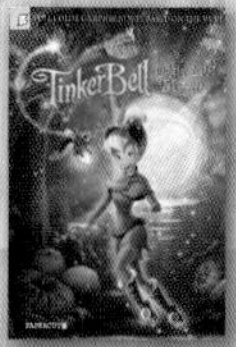

Graphic Novel #12
"Tinker Bell and the Lost Treasure"

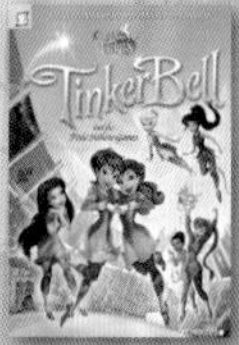

Graphic Novel #13
"Tinker Bell and the Pixie Hollow Games"

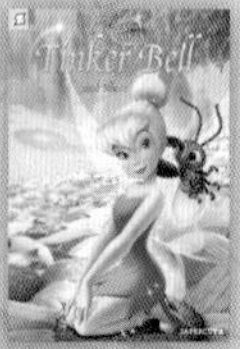

Graphic Novel #14
"Tinker Bell and Blaze"

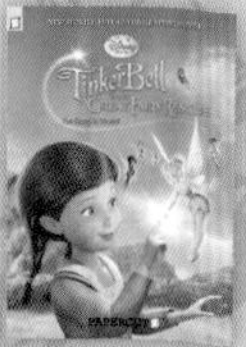

Tinker Bell and the Great Fairy Rescue

COMING SOON

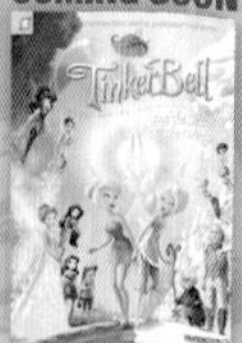

Graphic Novel #15
"Tinker Bell and the Secret of the Wings"

DISNEY FAIRIES graphic novels are available in paperback for $7.99 each; in hardcover for $12.99 each except #5, $6.99PB, $10.99HC. #6-15 are $7.99PB $11.99HC. Tinker Bell and the Great Fairy Rescue is $9.99 in hardcover only.
Available at booksellers everywhere.

See more at papercutz.com

Or you can order from us: Please add $4.00 for postage and handling for first book, and add $1.00 for each additional book. Please make check payable to NBM Publishing. Send to: Papercutz, 160 Broadway, Suite 700, East Wing, New York, NY 10038 or call 800 886 1223 (9-6 EST M-F) MC-Visa-Amex accepted.

DISNEY FAIRIES

#4 "Tinker Bell to the Rescue"

Contents

PAPERCUTZ™

NEW YORK

"Tinker Bell in Trouble"
Script: Paola Mulazzi
Revised Dialogue: Cortney Faye Powell
Layout: Emilio Urbano
Inks: Roberta Zanotta
Color: Stefania Santi
Page 5 Art:
Pencils: Manuela Razzi and Emilio Urbano
Inks: Marina Baggio
Color: Andrea Cagol

"Vidia is Kidnapped"
Script: Giulia Conti
Revised Dialogue: Calista Brill
Layout: Emilio Urbano
Clean up: Manuela Razzi
Inks: Roberta Zanotta
Color: Stefania Santi
Page 18 Art:
Pencils and Inks: Elisabetta Melaranci
Color: Andrea Cagol

"Tinker Bell Goes Batty!"
Script: Paola Mulazzi
Revised Dialogue: Cortney Faye Powell
Layout and Clean up: Elisabetta Melaranci
Inks: Marina Baggio
Color: Stefania Santi
Page 31 Art:
Layout: Emilio Urbano and Manuela Razzi
Pencils: Emilio Urbano
Inks: Marina Baggio
Color: Andrea Cagol

"If You Don't Have Anything Nice to Say…"
Script: Augusto Machetto
Revised Dialogue: Cortney Faye Powell
Layout and Clean up: Roberta Zanotta
Inks: Roberta Zanotta
Color: Stefania Santi
Page 44 Art:
Pencils and Inks: Elisabetta Melaranci
Color: Andrea Cagol

"Thistle's Last Scheme"
Script: Paola Mulazzi
Revised Dialogue: Cortney Faye Powell
Layout and Pencils: Gianluca Barone
Clean up: Caterina Giorgetti
Inks: Marina Baggio
Color: Stefanie Santi
Page 57 Art:
Pencils and Inks: Elisabetta Melaranci
Color: Andrea Cagol

Chris Nelson and Caitlin Hinrichs – Production
Beth Scorzato – Production Coordinator
Michael Petranek – Associate Editor
Jim Salicrup – Editor-in-Chief

ISBN: 978-1-59707-200-7 paperback edition
ISBN: 978-1-59707-230-4 hardcover edition

Printed in China
May 2014 by Asia One Printing LTD
13/F Asia One Tower
8 Fung Yip St., Chaiwan, Hong Kong

Papercutz books maye be purchased for business or promtional use.
For information on bulk purchases please contact Macmillan Corporate and Premium
Sales Department at (800) 221-7945 x5442

Distributed by Macmillan.

Third Papercutz Printing

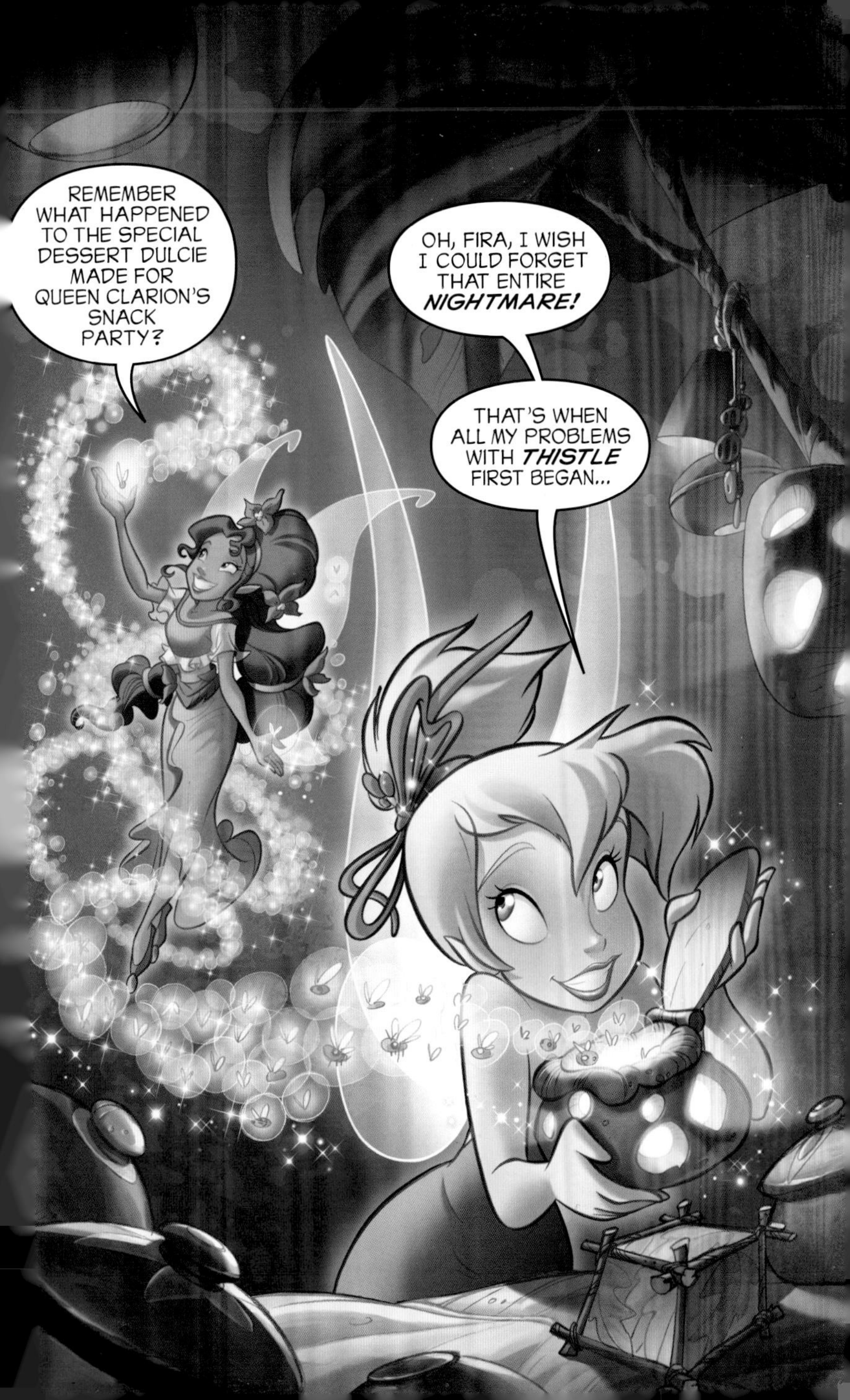
REMEMBER WHAT HAPPENED TO THE SPECIAL DESSERT DULCIE MADE FOR QUEEN CLARION'S SNACK PARTY?
OH, FIRA, I WISH I COULD FORGET THAT ENTIRE NIGHTMARE!
THAT'S WHEN ALL MY PROBLEMS WITH THISTLE FIRST BEGAN...

TINKER BELL IN TROUBLE

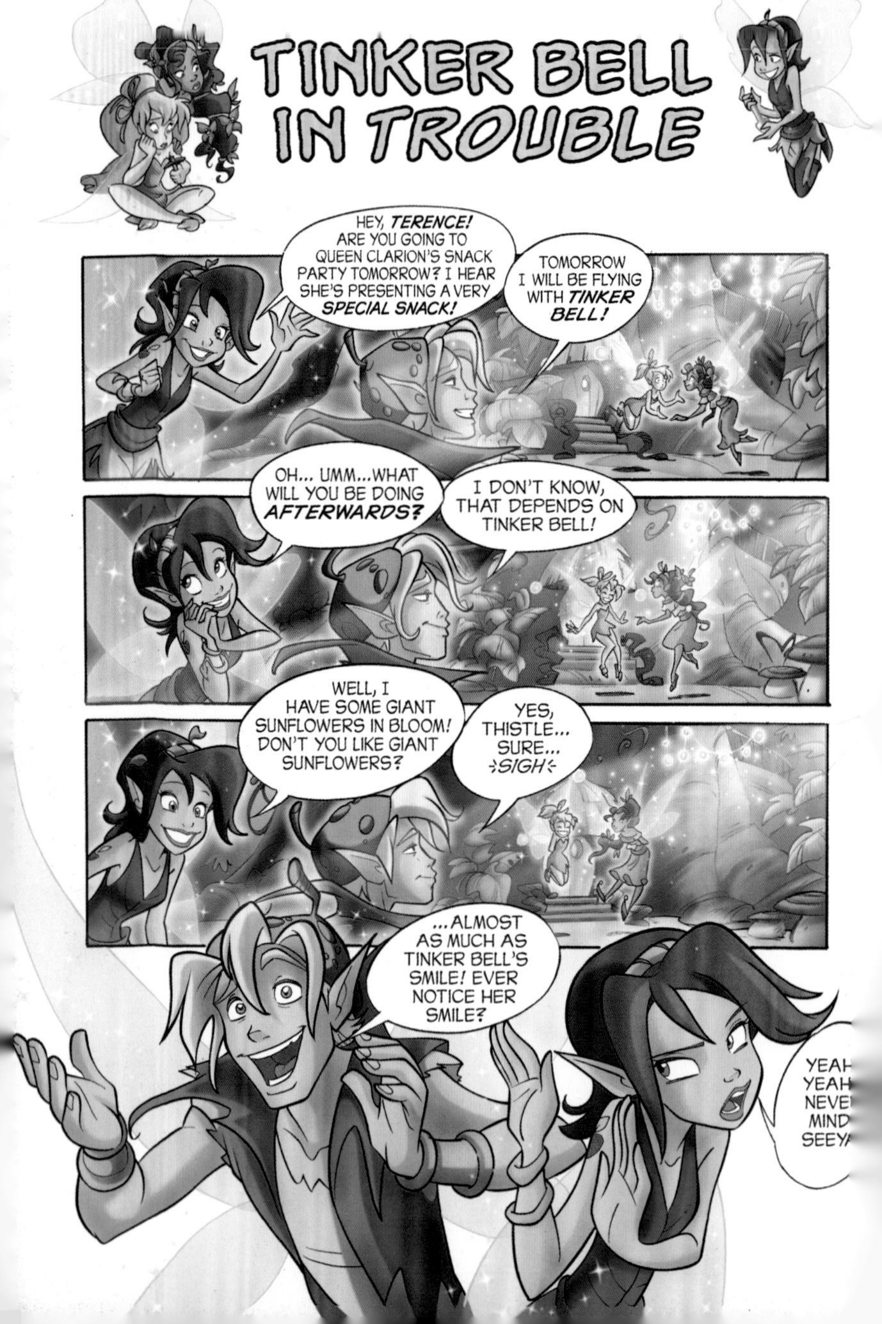
HEY, TERENCE! ARE YOU GOING TO QUEEN CLARION'S SNACK PARTY TOMORROW? I HEAR SHE'S PRESENTING A VERY SPECIAL SNACK!
TOMORROW I WILL BE FLYING WITH TINKER BELL!
OH... UMM...WHAT WILL YOU BE DOING AFTERWARDS?
I DON'T KNOW, THAT DEPENDS ON TINKER BELL!
WELL, I HAVE SOME GIANT SUNFLOWERS IN BLOOM! DON'T YOU LIKE GIANT SUNFLOWERS?
YES, THISTLE... SURE... SIGH
...ALMOST AS MUCH AS TINKER BELL'S SMILE! EVER NOTICE HER SMILE?
YEAH YEAH NEVE MIND SEEY

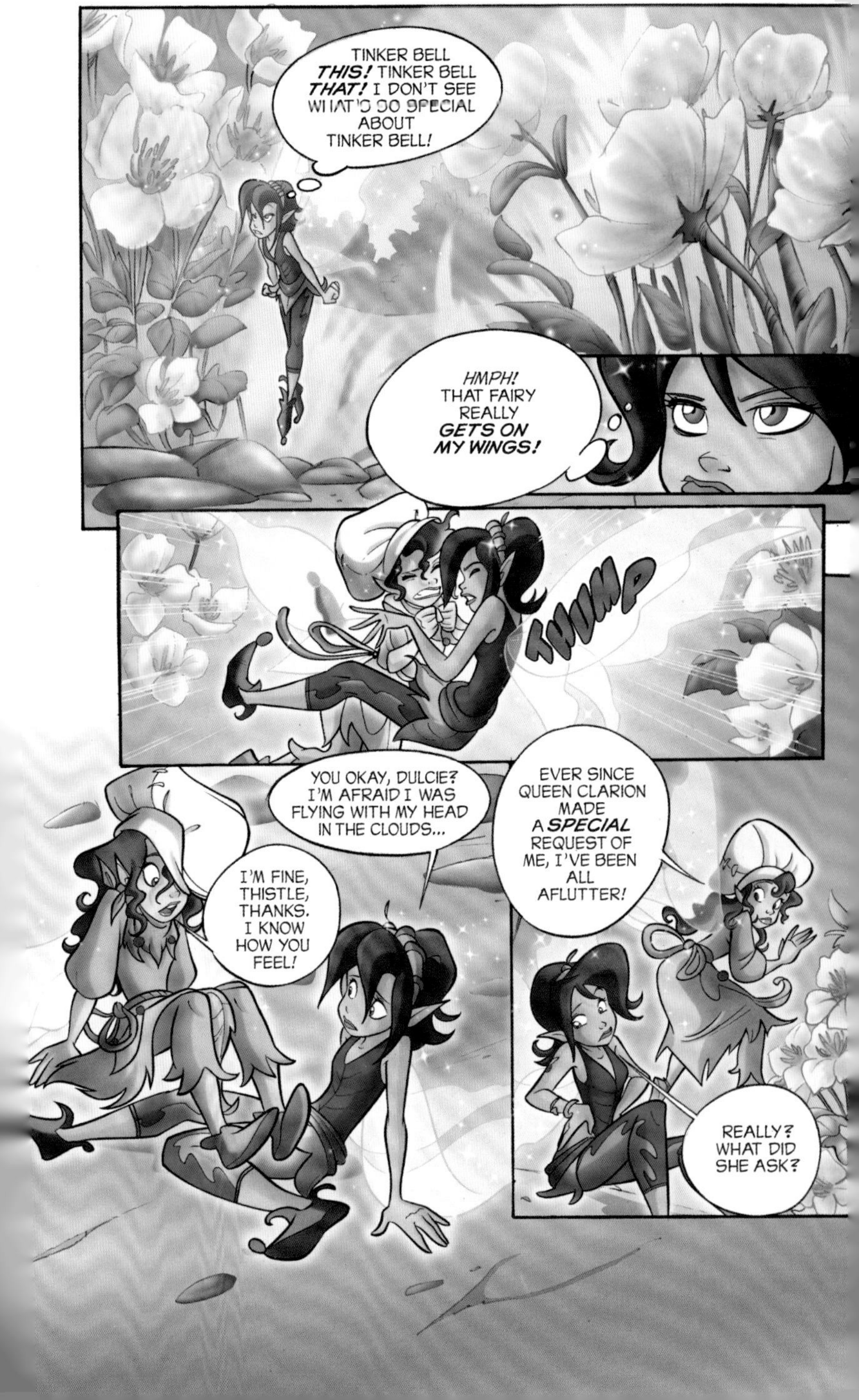
TINKER BELL THIS! TINKER BELL THAT! I DON'T SEE WHAT'S SO SPECIAL ABOUT TINKER BELL!
HMPH! THAT FAIRY REALLY GETS ON MY WINGS!
THUMP
YOU OKAY, DULCIE? I'M AFRAID I WAS FLYING WITH MY HEAD IN THE CLOUDS...
I'M FINE, THISTLE, THANKS. I KNOW HOW YOU FEEL!
EVER SINCE QUEEN CLARION MADE A SPECIAL REQUEST OF ME, I'VE BEEN ALL AFLUTTER!
REALLY? WHAT DID SHE ASK?

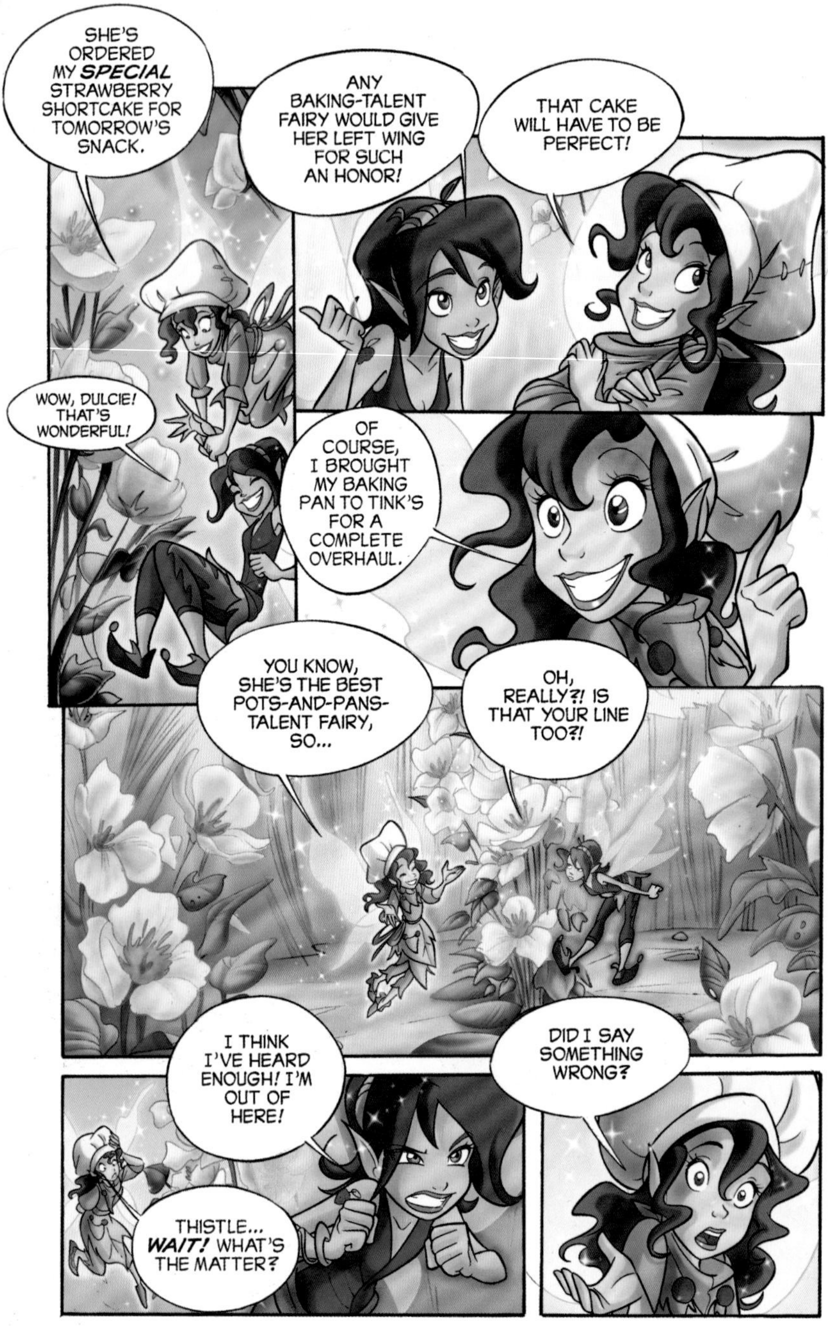
SHE'S ORDERED MY SPECIAL STRAWBERRY SHORTCAKE FOR TOMORROW'S SNACK.
ANY BAKING-TALENT FAIRY WOULD GIVE HER LEFT WING FOR SUCH AN HONOR!
THAT CAKE WILL HAVE TO BE PERFECT!
WOW, DULCIE! THAT'S WONDERFUL!
OF COURSE, I BROUGHT MY BAKING PAN TO TINK'S FOR A COMPLETE OVERHAUL.
YOU KNOW, SHE'S THE BEST POTS-AND-PANS-TALENT FAIRY, SO...
OH, REALLY?! IS THAT YOUR LINE TOO?!
I THINK I'VE HEARD ENOUGH! I'M OUT OF HERE!
DID I SAY SOMETHING WRONG?
THISTLE... WAIT! WHAT'S THE MATTER?

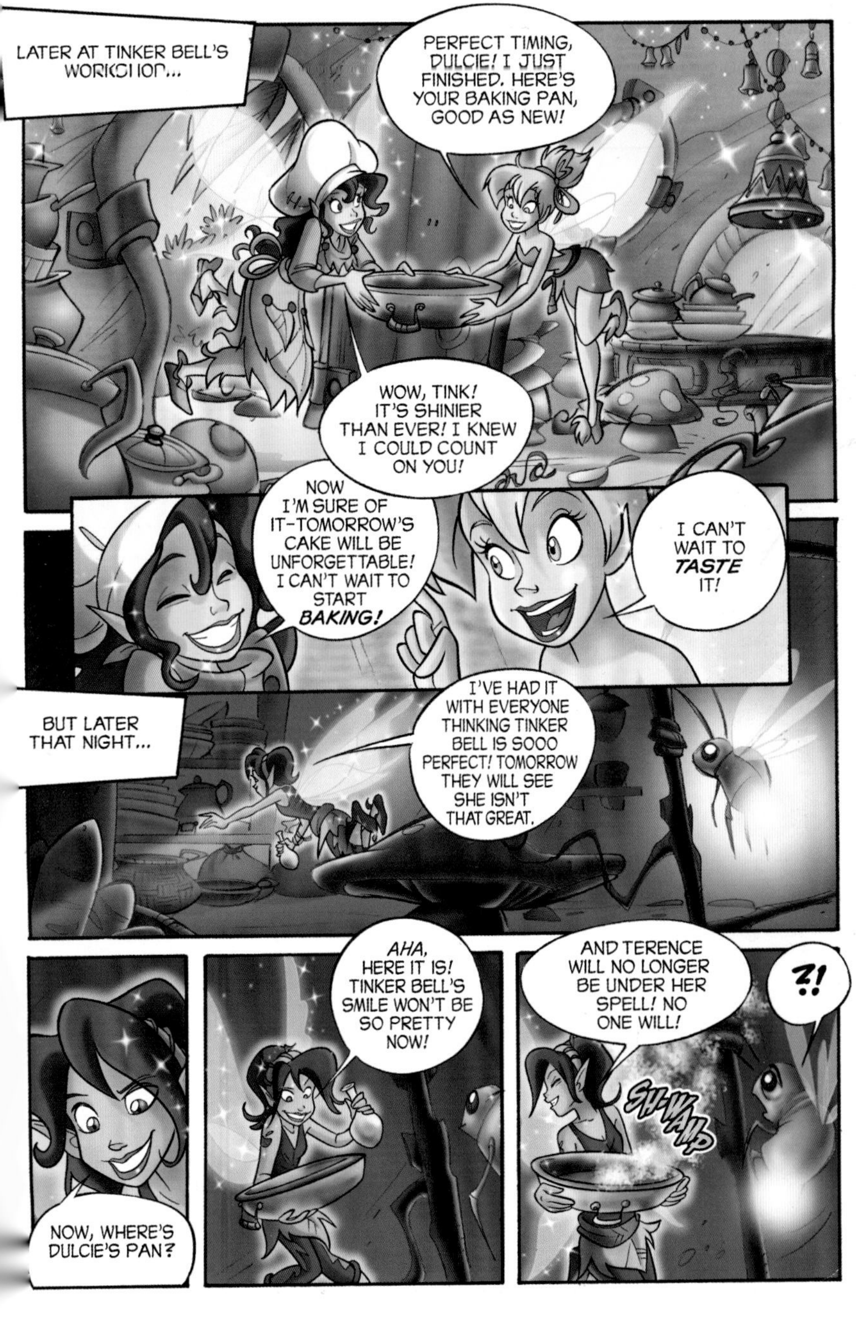
LATER AT TINKER BELL'S WORKSHOP...
PERFECT TIMING, DULCIE! I JUST FINISHED. HERE'S YOUR BAKING PAN, GOOD AS NEW!
WOW, TINK! IT'S SHINIER THAN EVER! I KNEW I COULD COUNT ON YOU!
NOW I'M SURE OF IT–TOMORROW'S CAKE WILL BE UNFORGETTABLE! I CAN'T WAIT TO START BAKING!
I CAN'T WAIT TO TASTE IT!
BUT LATER THAT NIGHT...
I'VE HAD IT WITH EVERYONE THINKING TINKER BELL IS SOOO PERFECT! TOMORROW THEY WILL SEE SHE ISN'T THAT GREAT.
NOW, WHERE'S DULCIE'S PAN?
AHA, HERE IT IS! TINKER BELL'S SMILE WON'T BE SO PRETTY NOW!
AND TERENCE WILL NO LONGER BE UNDER HER SPELL! NO ONE WILL!
SH-WAMP
?!

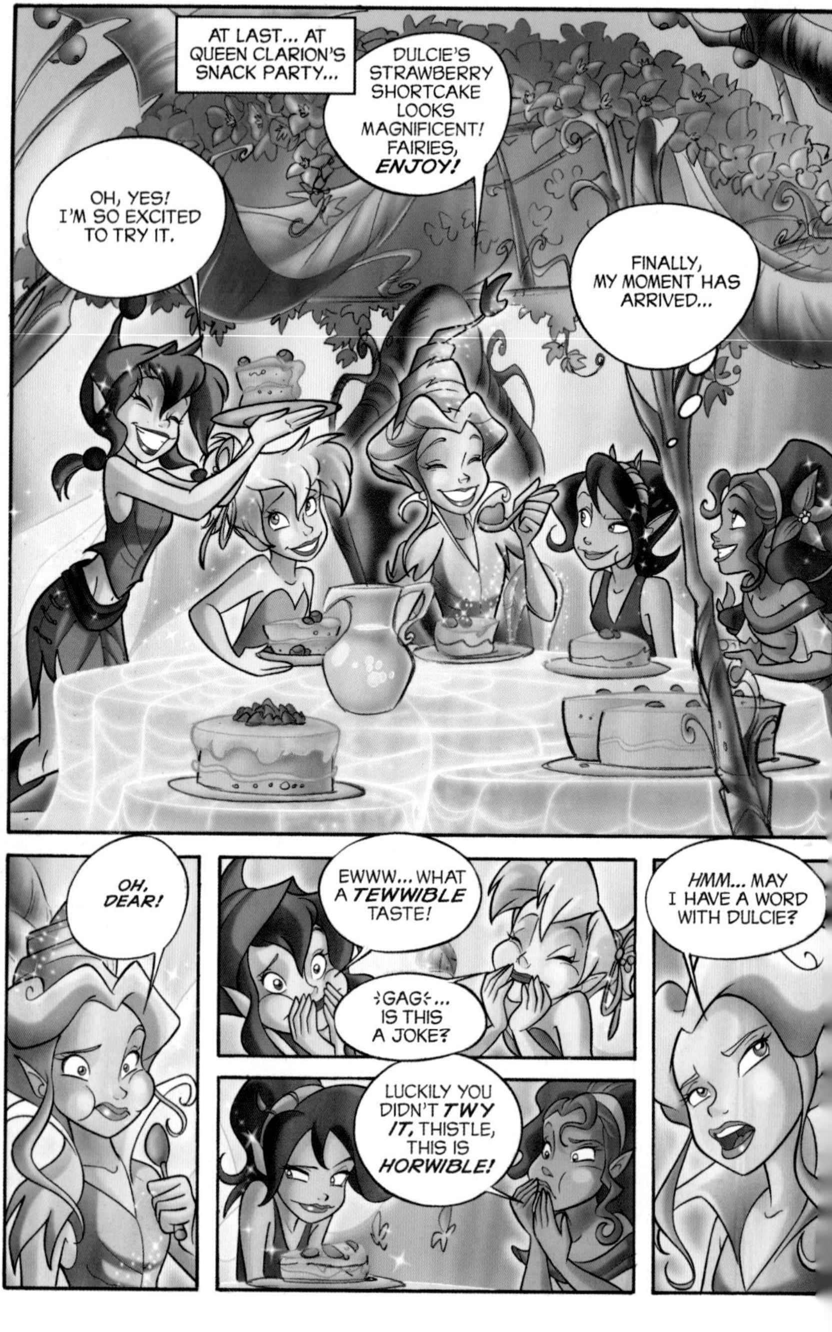
AT LAST... AT QUEEN CLARION'S SNACK PARTY...
DULCIE'S STRAWBERRY SHORTCAKE LOOKS MAGNIFICENT! FAIRIES, ENJOY!
OH, YES! I'M SO EXCITED TO TRY IT.
FINALLY, MY MOMENT HAS ARRIVED...
OH, DEAR!
EWWW... WHAT A TEWWIBLE TASTE!
⁑GAG⁑... IS THIS A JOKE?
LUCKILY YOU DIDN'T TWY IT, THISTLE, THIS IS HORWIBLE!
HMM... MAY I HAVE A WORD WITH DULCIE?

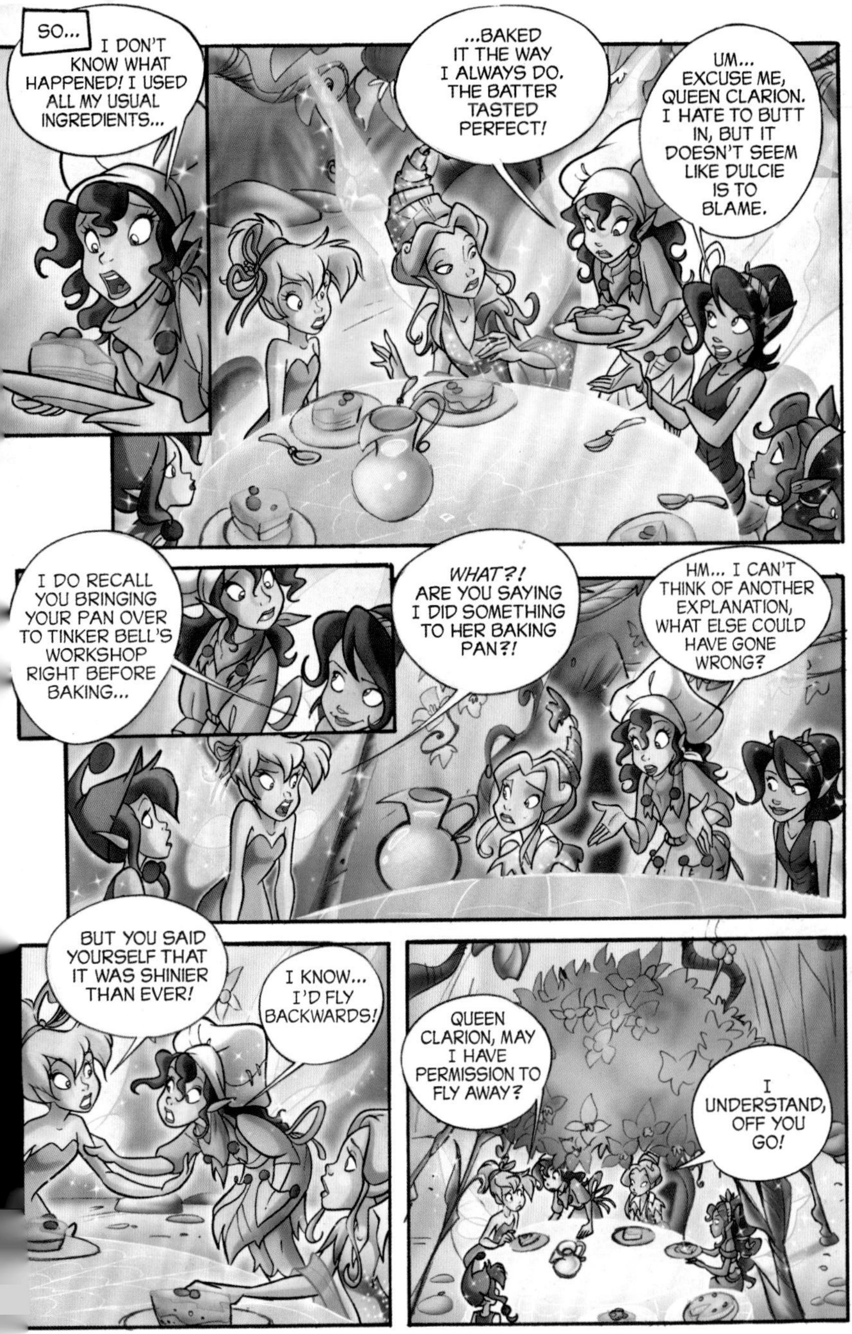
SO...
I DON'T KNOW WHAT HAPPENED! I USED ALL MY USUAL INGREDIENTS...
...BAKED IT THE WAY I ALWAYS DO. THE BATTER TASTED PERFECT!
UM... EXCUSE ME, QUEEN CLARION. I HATE TO BUTT IN, BUT IT DOESN'T SEEM LIKE DULCIE IS TO BLAME.
I DO RECALL YOU BRINGING YOUR PAN OVER TO TINKER BELL'S WORKSHOP RIGHT BEFORE BAKING...
WHAT?! ARE YOU SAYING I DID SOMETHING TO HER BAKING PAN?!
HM... I CAN'T THINK OF ANOTHER EXPLANATION, WHAT ELSE COULD HAVE GONE WRONG?
BUT YOU SAID YOURSELF THAT IT WAS SHINIER THAN EVER!
I KNOW... I'D FLY BACKWARDS!
QUEEN CLARION, MAY I HAVE PERMISSION TO FLY AWAY?
I UNDERSTAND, OFF YOU GO!

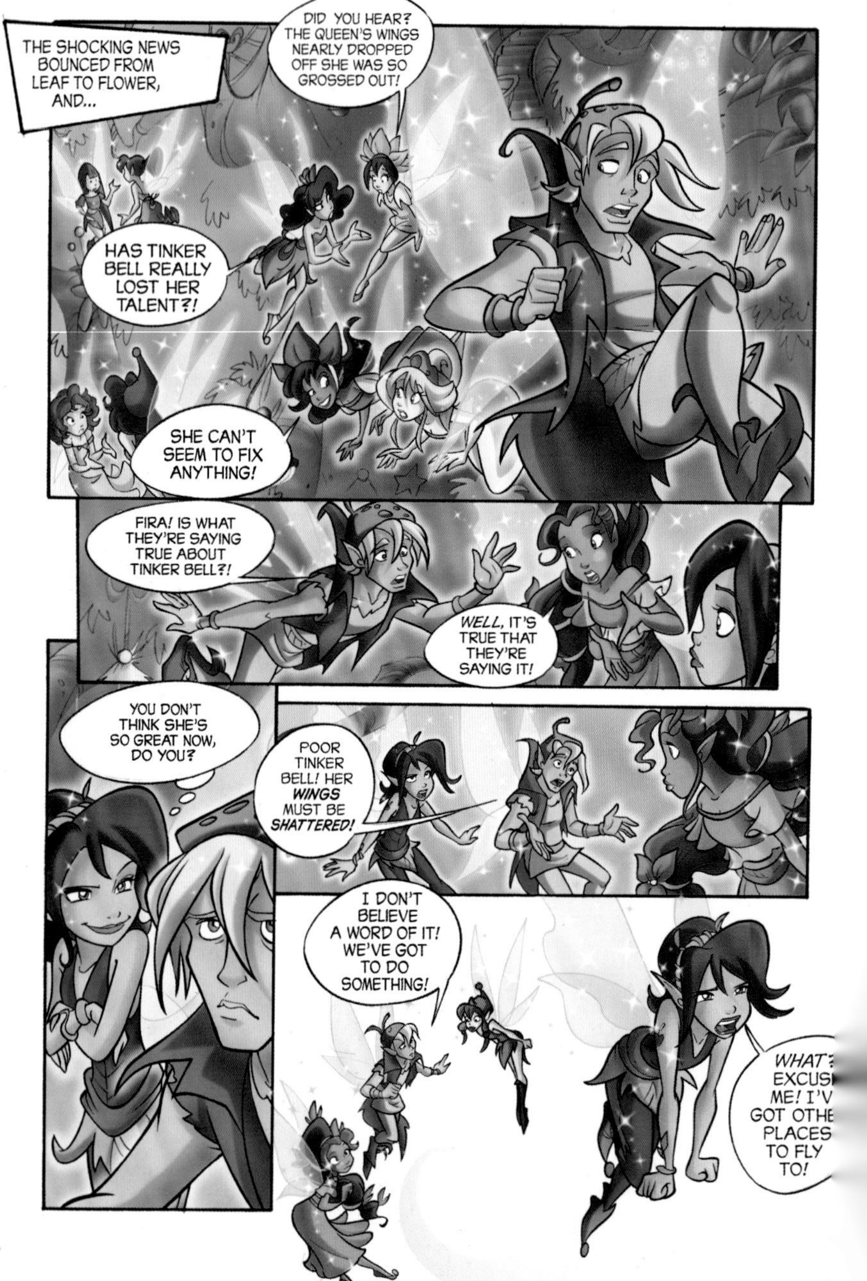
THE SHOCKING NEWS BOUNCED FROM LEAF TO FLOWER, AND...
DID YOU HEAR? THE QUEEN'S WINGS NEARLY DROPPED OFF SHE WAS SO GROSSED OUT!
HAS TINKER BELL REALLY LOST HER TALENT?!
SHE CAN'T SEEM TO FIX ANYTHING!
FIRA! IS WHAT THEY'RE SAYING TRUE ABOUT TINKER BELL?!
WELL, IT'S TRUE THAT THEY'RE SAYING IT!
YOU DON'T THINK SHE'S SO GREAT NOW, DO YOU?
POOR TINKER BELL! HER WINGS MUST BE SHATTERED!
I DON'T BELIEVE A WORD OF IT! WE'VE GOT TO DO SOMETHING!
WHAT?
EXCUS
ME! I'V
GOT OTHE
PLACES
TO FLY
TO!

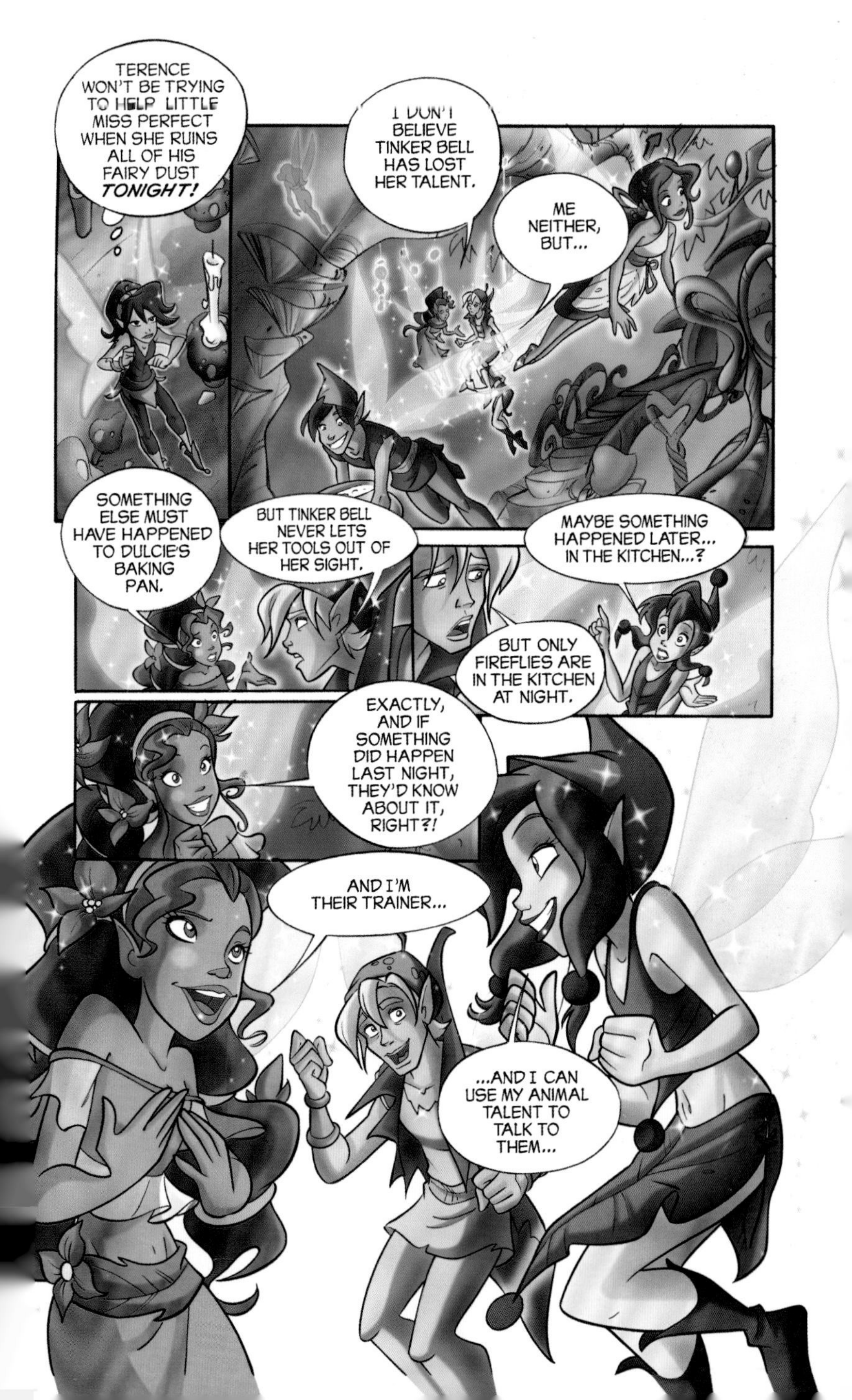
TERENCE WON'T BE TRYING TO HELP LITTLE MISS PERFECT WHEN SHE RUINS ALL OF HIS FAIRY DUST *TONIGHT!*
I DON'T BELIEVE TINKER BELL HAS LOST HER TALENT.
ME NEITHER, BUT...
SOMETHING ELSE MUST HAVE HAPPENED TO DULCIE'S BAKING PAN.
BUT TINKER BELL NEVER LETS HER TOOLS OUT OF HER SIGHT.
MAYBE SOMETHING HAPPENED LATER... IN THE KITCHEN...?
BUT ONLY FIREFLIES ARE IN THE KITCHEN AT NIGHT.
EXACTLY, AND IF SOMETHING DID HAPPEN LAST NIGHT, THEY'D KNOW ABOUT IT, RIGHT?!
AND I'M THEIR TRAINER...
...AND I CAN USE MY ANIMAL TALENT TO TALK TO THEM...

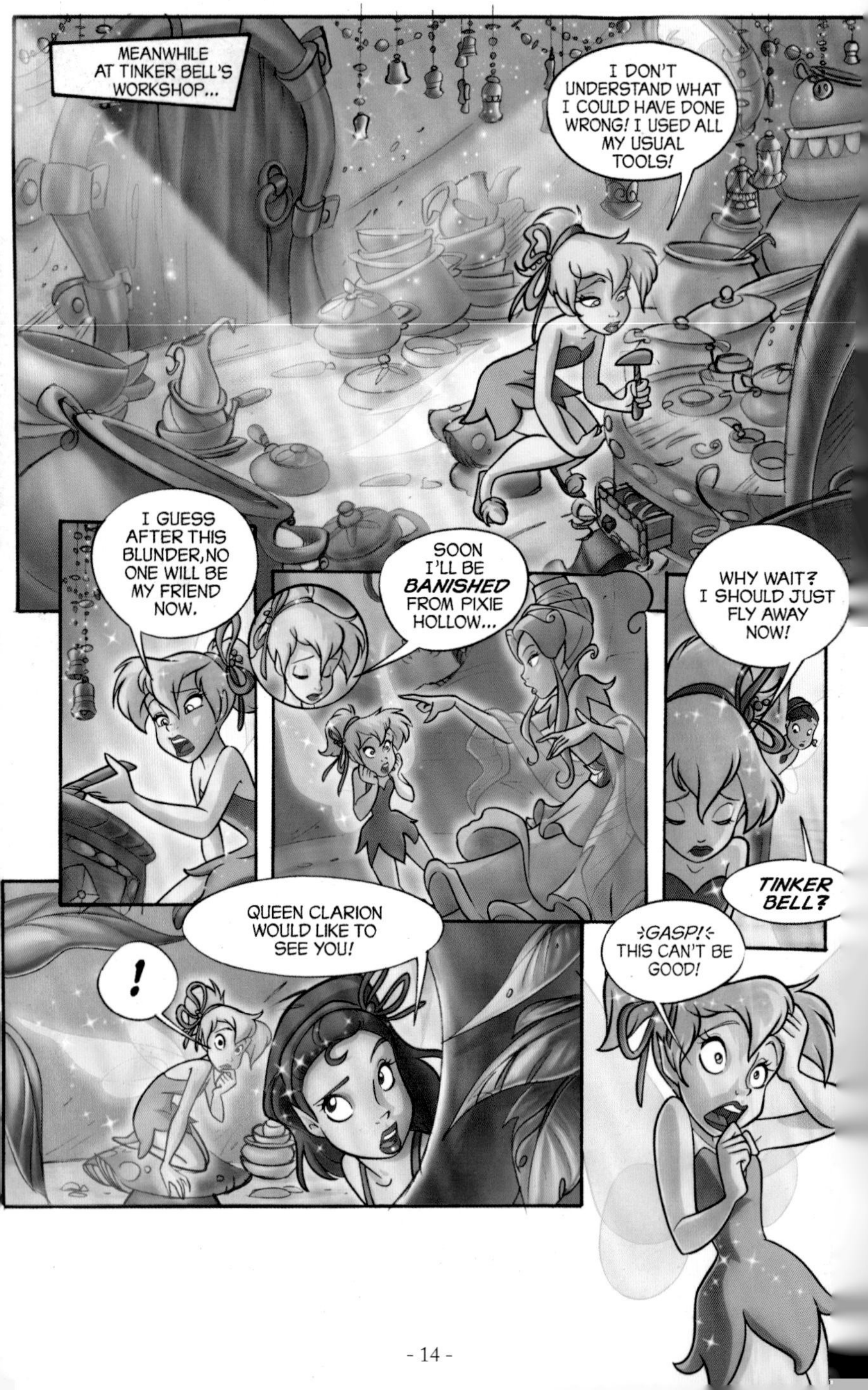
MEANWHILE AT TINKER BELL'S WORKSHOP...
I DON'T UNDERSTAND WHAT I COULD HAVE DONE WRONG! I USED ALL MY USUAL TOOLS!
I GUESS AFTER THIS BLUNDER, NO ONE WILL BE MY FRIEND NOW.
SOON I'LL BE BANISHED FROM PIXIE HOLLOW...
WHY WAIT? I SHOULD JUST FLY AWAY NOW!
TINKER BELL?
QUEEN CLARION WOULD LIKE TO SEE YOU!
!
GASP! THIS CAN'T BE GOOD!

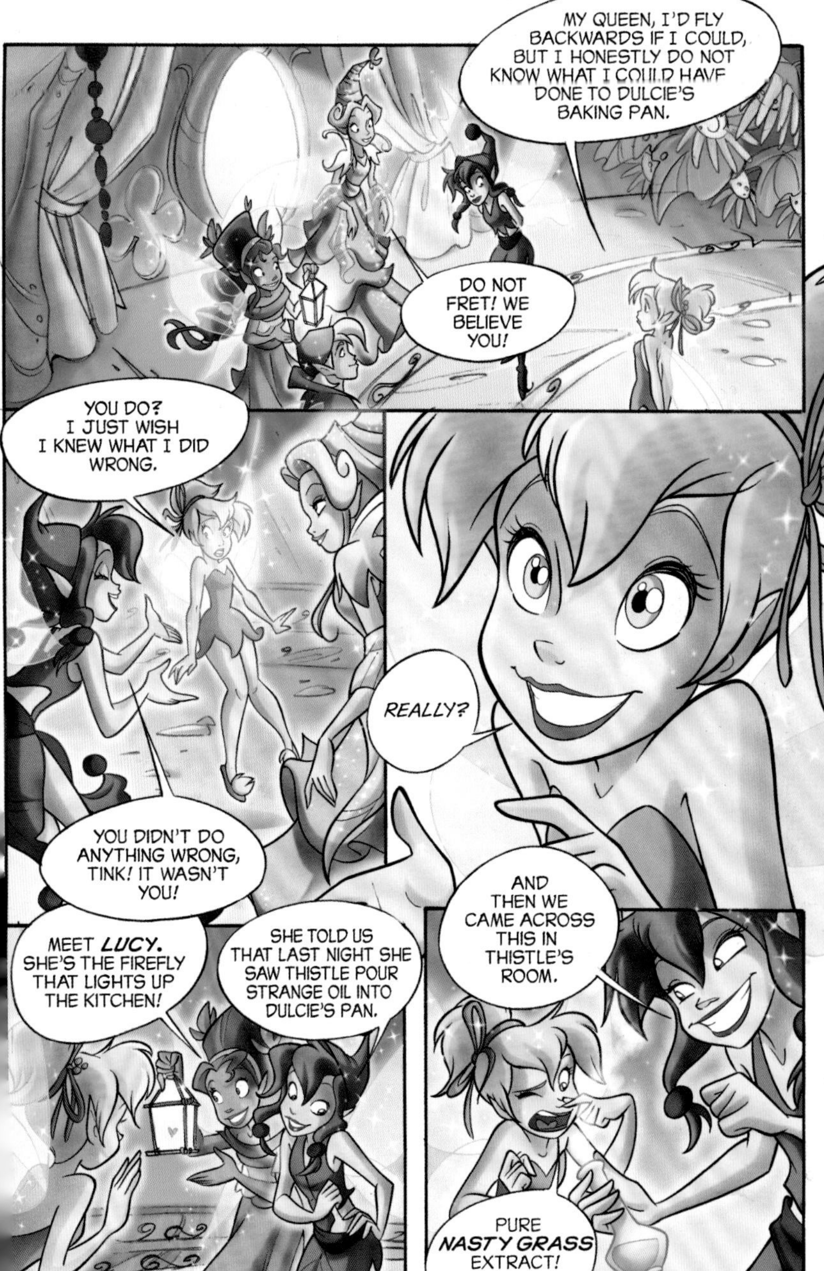

MY QUEEN, I'D FLY BACKWARDS IF I COULD, BUT I HONESTLY DO NOT KNOW WHAT I COULD HAVE DONE TO DULCIE'S BAKING PAN.
DO NOT FRET! WE BELIEVE YOU!
YOU DO? I JUST WISH I KNEW WHAT I DID WRONG.
YOU DIDN'T DO ANYTHING WRONG, TINK! IT WASN'T YOU!
REALLY?
MEET LUCY. SHE'S THE FIREFLY THAT LIGHTS UP THE KITCHEN!
SHE TOLD US THAT LAST NIGHT SHE SAW THISTLE POUR STRANGE OIL INTO DULCIE'S PAN.
AND THEN WE CAME ACROSS THIS IN THISTLE'S ROOM.
PURE NASTY GRASS EXTRACT! YUCK!

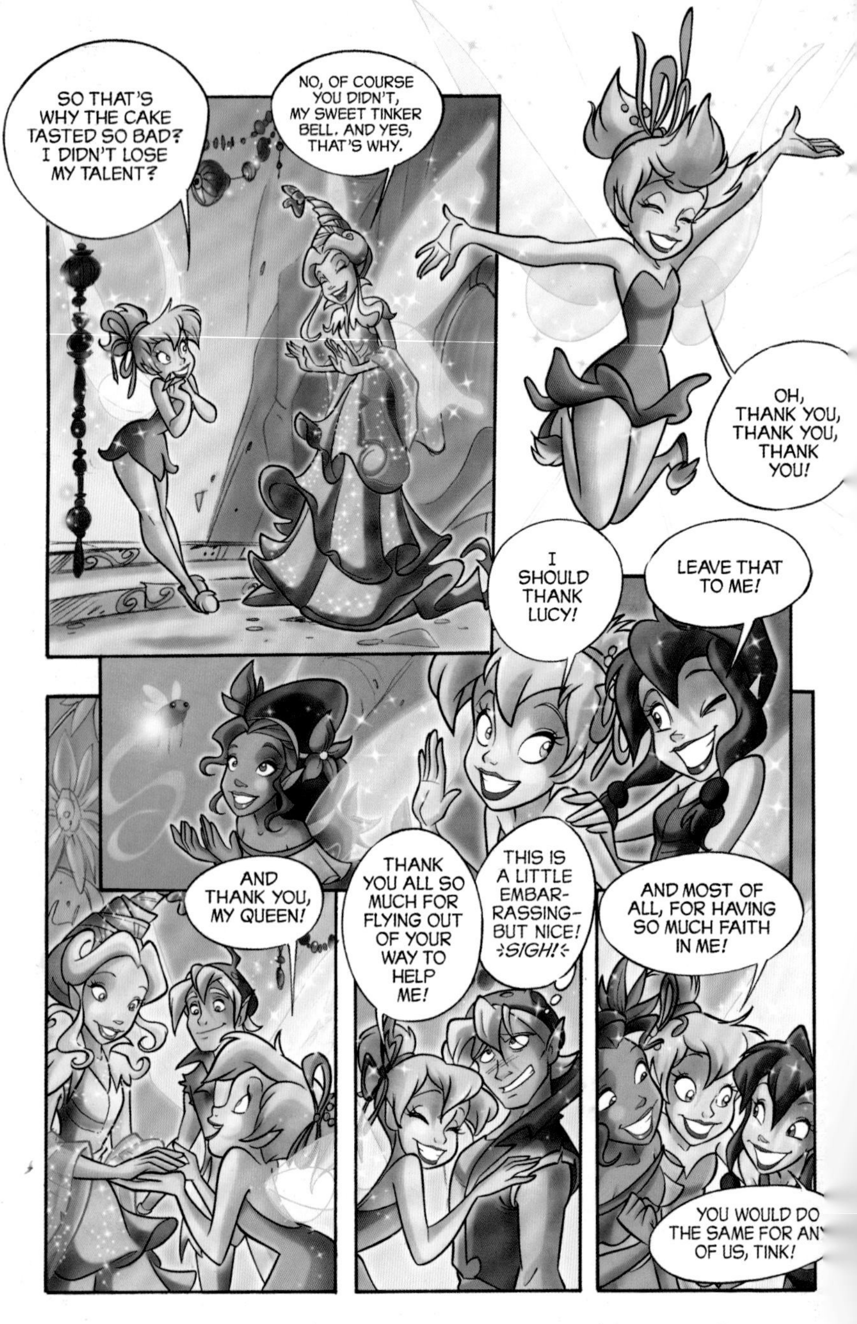
SO THAT'S WHY THE CAKE TASTED SO BAD? I DIDN'T LOSE MY TALENT?
NO, OF COURSE YOU DIDN'T, MY SWEET TINKER BELL. AND YES, THAT'S WHY.
OH, THANK YOU, THANK YOU, THANK YOU!
I SHOULD THANK LUCY!
LEAVE THAT TO ME!
AND THANK YOU, MY QUEEN!
THANK YOU ALL SO MUCH FOR FLYING OUT OF YOUR WAY TO HELP ME!
THIS IS A LITTLE EMBAR-RASSING- BUT NICE! SIGH!
AND MOST OF ALL, FOR HAVING SO MUCH FAITH IN ME!
YOU WOULD DO THE SAME FOR AN OF US, TINK!

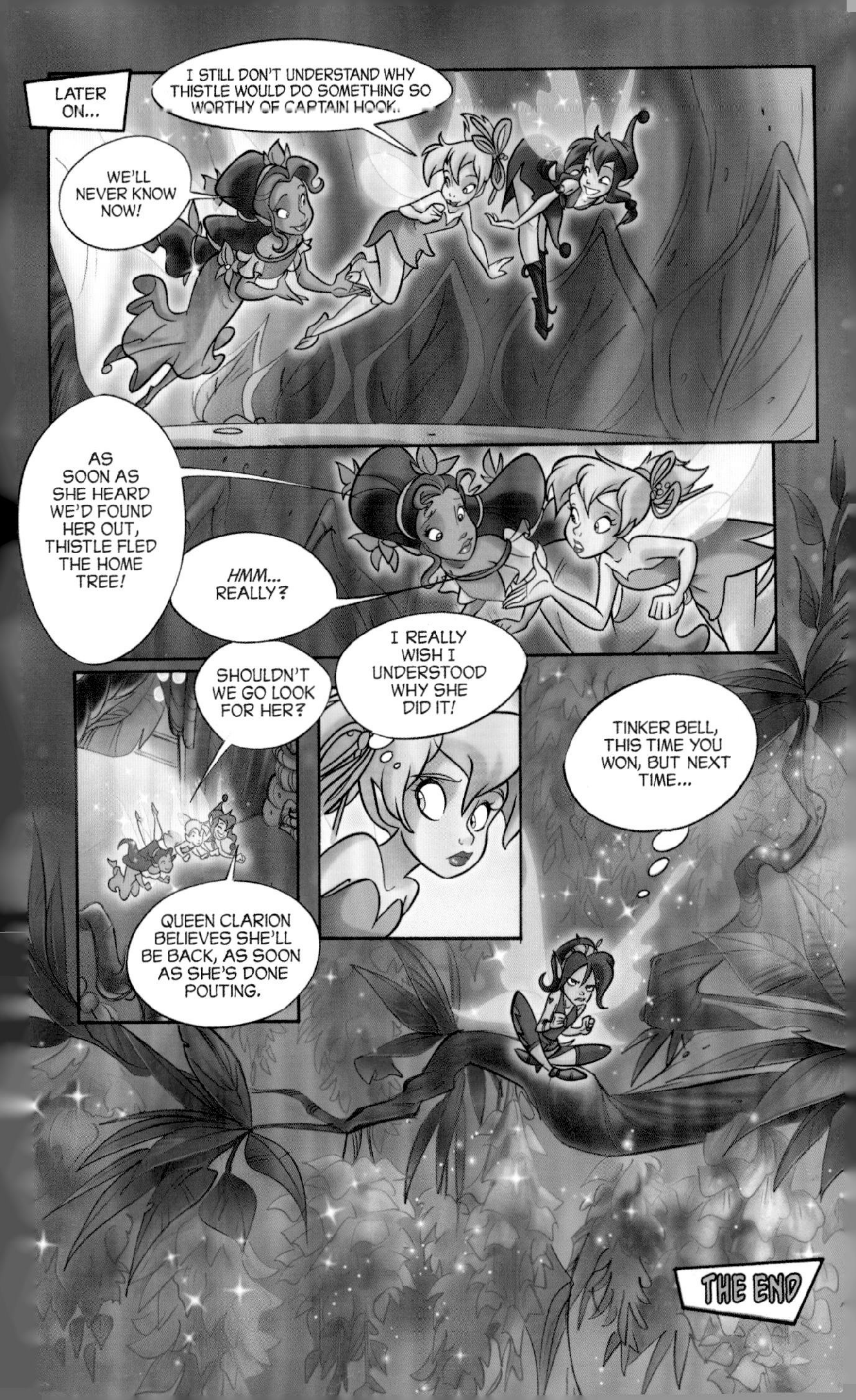
LATER ON...
I STILL DON'T UNDERSTAND WHY THISTLE WOULD DO SOMETHING SO WORTHY OF CAPTAIN HOOK.
WE'LL NEVER KNOW NOW!
AS SOON AS SHE HEARD WE'D FOUND HER OUT, THISTLE FLED THE HOME TREE!
HMM... REALLY?
SHOULDN'T WE GO LOOK FOR HER?
QUEEN CLARION BELIEVES SHE'LL BE BACK, AS SOON AS SHE'S DONE POUTING.
I REALLY WISH I UNDERSTOOD WHY SHE DID IT!
TINKER BELL, THIS TIME YOU WON, BUT NEXT TIME...
THE END

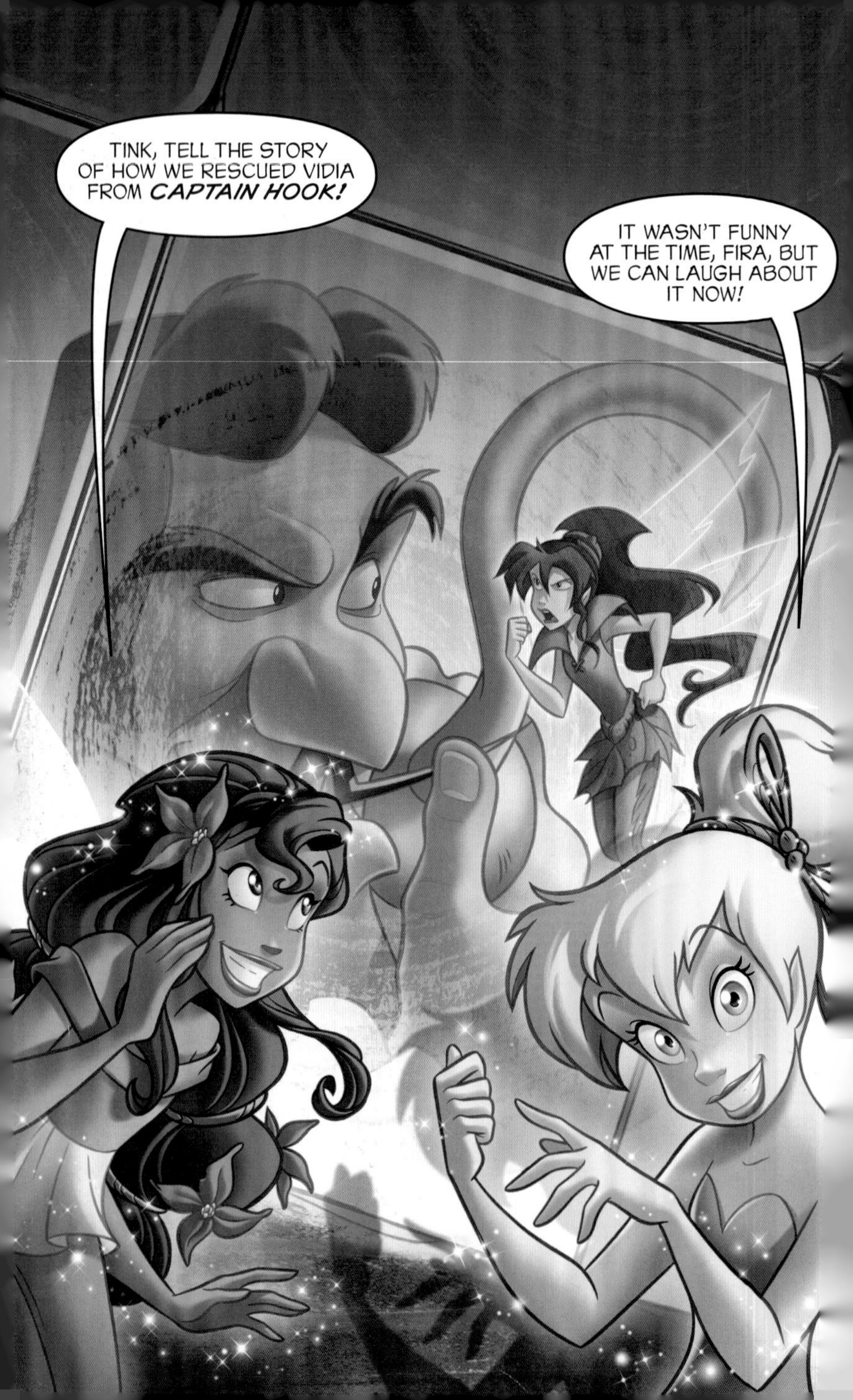
TINK, TELL THE STORY OF HOW WE RESCUED VIDIA FROM *CAPTAIN HOOK!*
IT WASN'T FUNNY AT THE TIME, FIRA, BUT WE CAN LAUGH ABOUT IT NOW!

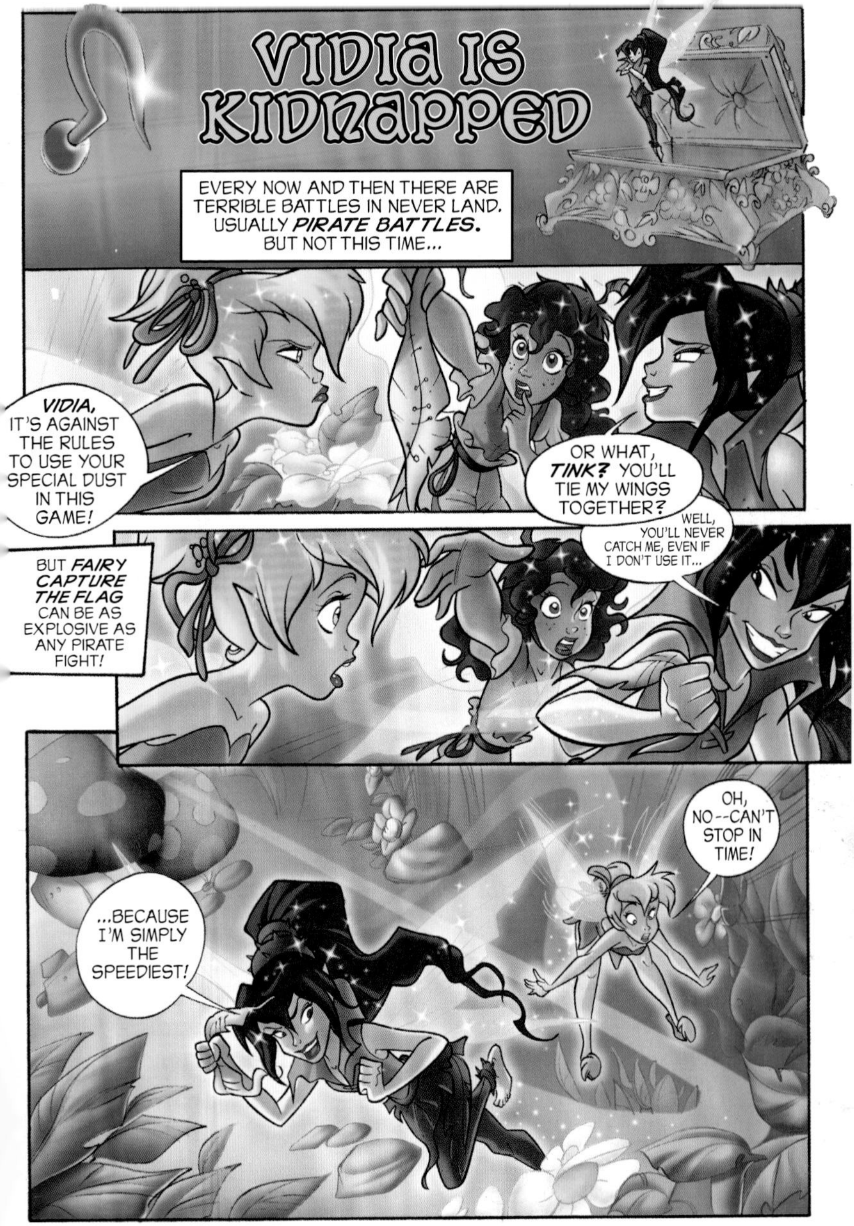
VIDIA IS KIDNAPPED
EVERY NOW AND THEN THERE ARE TERRIBLE BATTLES IN NEVER LAND. USUALLY PIRATE BATTLES. BUT NOT THIS TIME...
VIDIA, IT'S AGAINST THE RULES TO USE YOUR SPECIAL DUST IN THIS GAME!
OR WHAT, TINK? YOU'LL TIE MY WINGS TOGETHER?
WELL, YOU'LL NEVER CATCH ME, EVEN IF I DON'T USE IT...
BUT FAIRY CAPTURE THE FLAG CAN BE AS EXPLOSIVE AS ANY PIRATE FIGHT!
...BECAUSE I'M SIMPLY THE SPEEDIEST!
OH, NO--CAN'T STOP IN TIME!

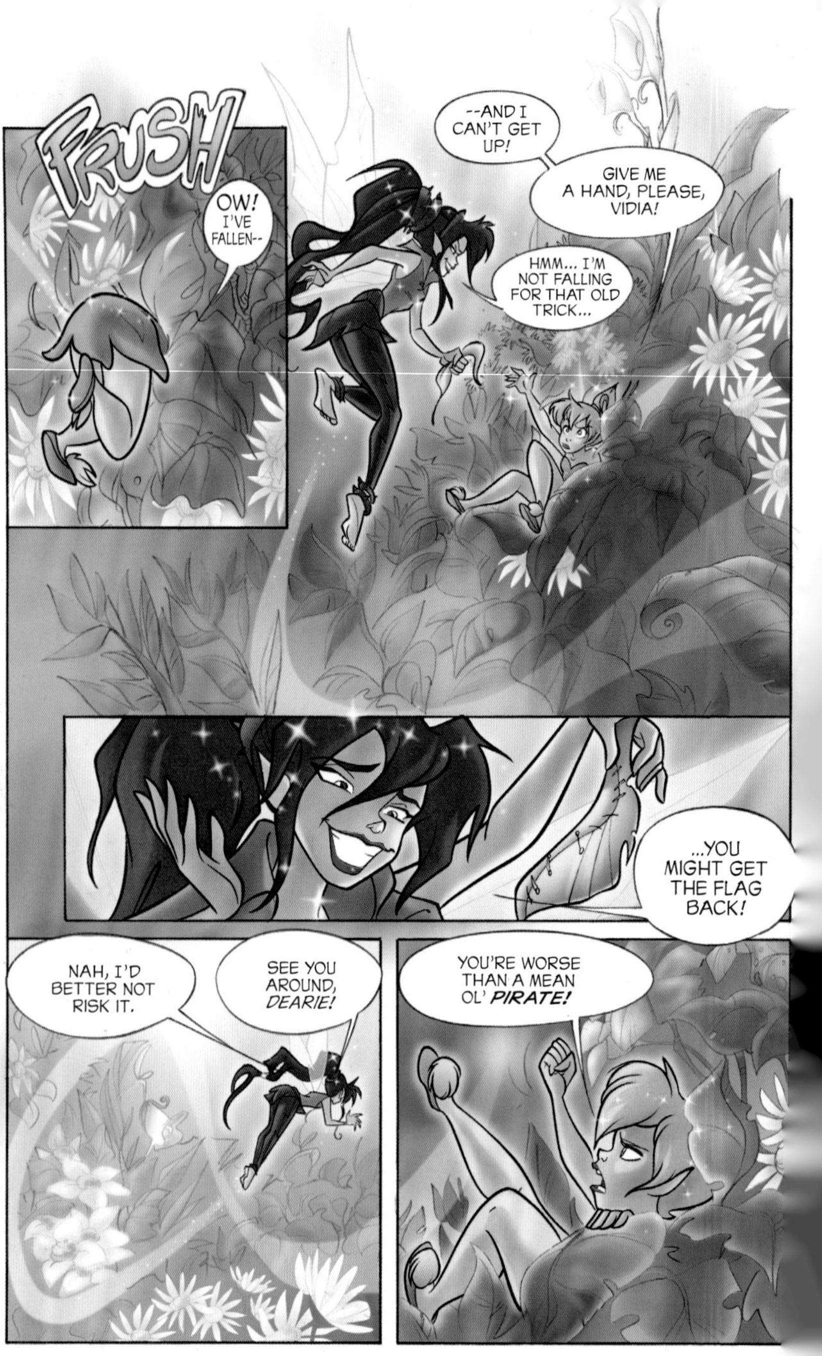
PRUSH
OW! I'VE FALLEN--
--AND I CAN'T GET UP!
GIVE ME A HAND, PLEASE, VIDIA!
HMM... I'M NOT FALLING FOR THAT OLD TRICK...
...YOU MIGHT GET THE FLAG BACK!
NAH, I'D BETTER NOT RISK IT.
SEE YOU AROUND, *DEARIE!*
YOU'RE WORSE THAN A MEAN OL' ***PIRATE!***

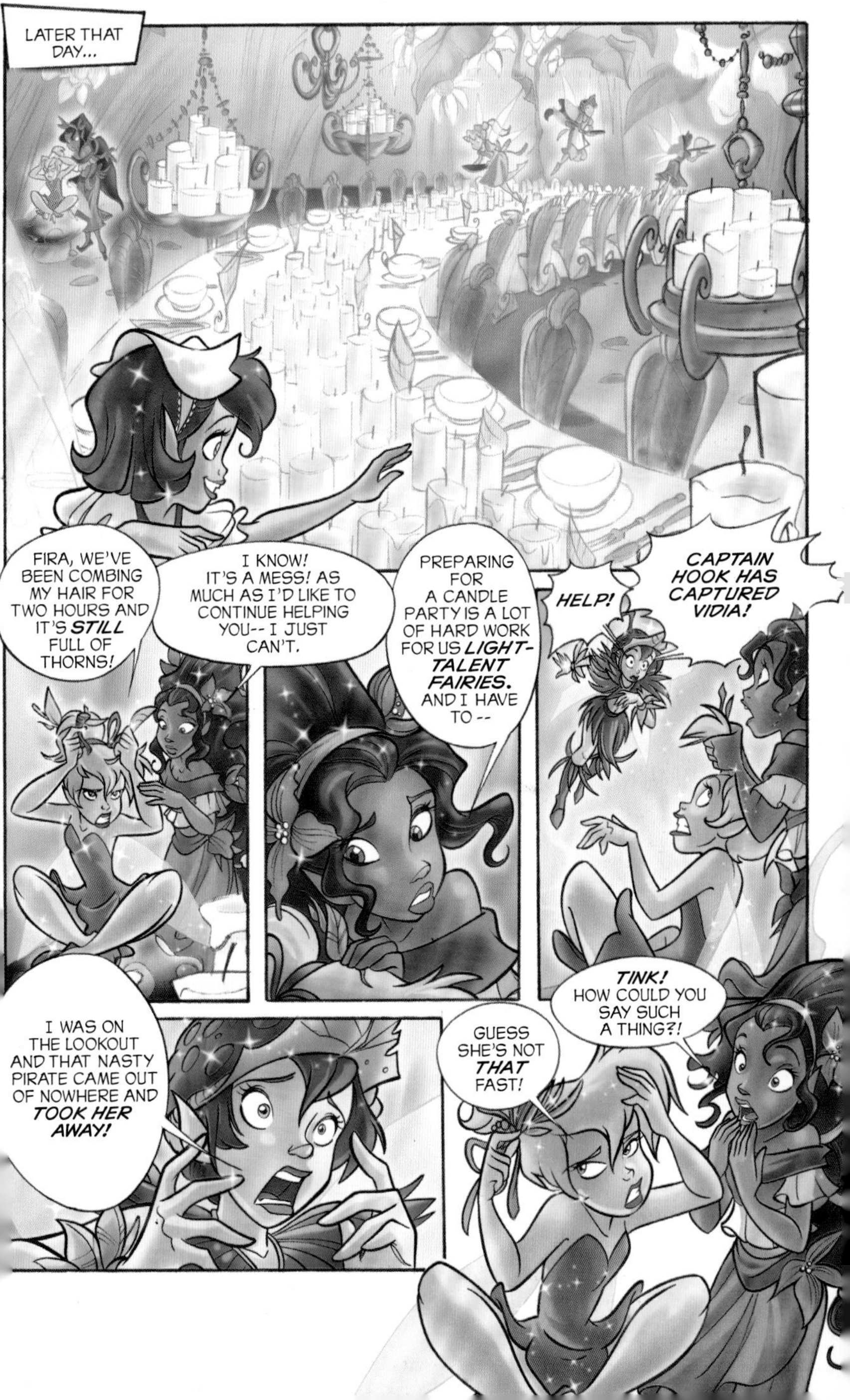
LATER THAT DAY...
FIRA, WE'VE BEEN COMBING MY HAIR FOR TWO HOURS AND IT'S STILL FULL OF THORNS!
I KNOW! IT'S A MESS! AS MUCH AS I'D LIKE TO CONTINUE HELPING YOU-- I JUST CAN'T.
PREPARING FOR A CANDLE PARTY IS A LOT OF HARD WORK FOR US LIGHT-TALENT FAIRIES. AND I HAVE TO --
HELP!
CAPTAIN HOOK HAS CAPTURED VIDIA!
I WAS ON THE LOOKOUT AND THAT NASTY PIRATE CAME OUT OF NOWHERE AND TOOK HER AWAY!
GUESS SHE'S NOT THAT FAST!
TINK! HOW COULD YOU SAY SUCH A THING?!

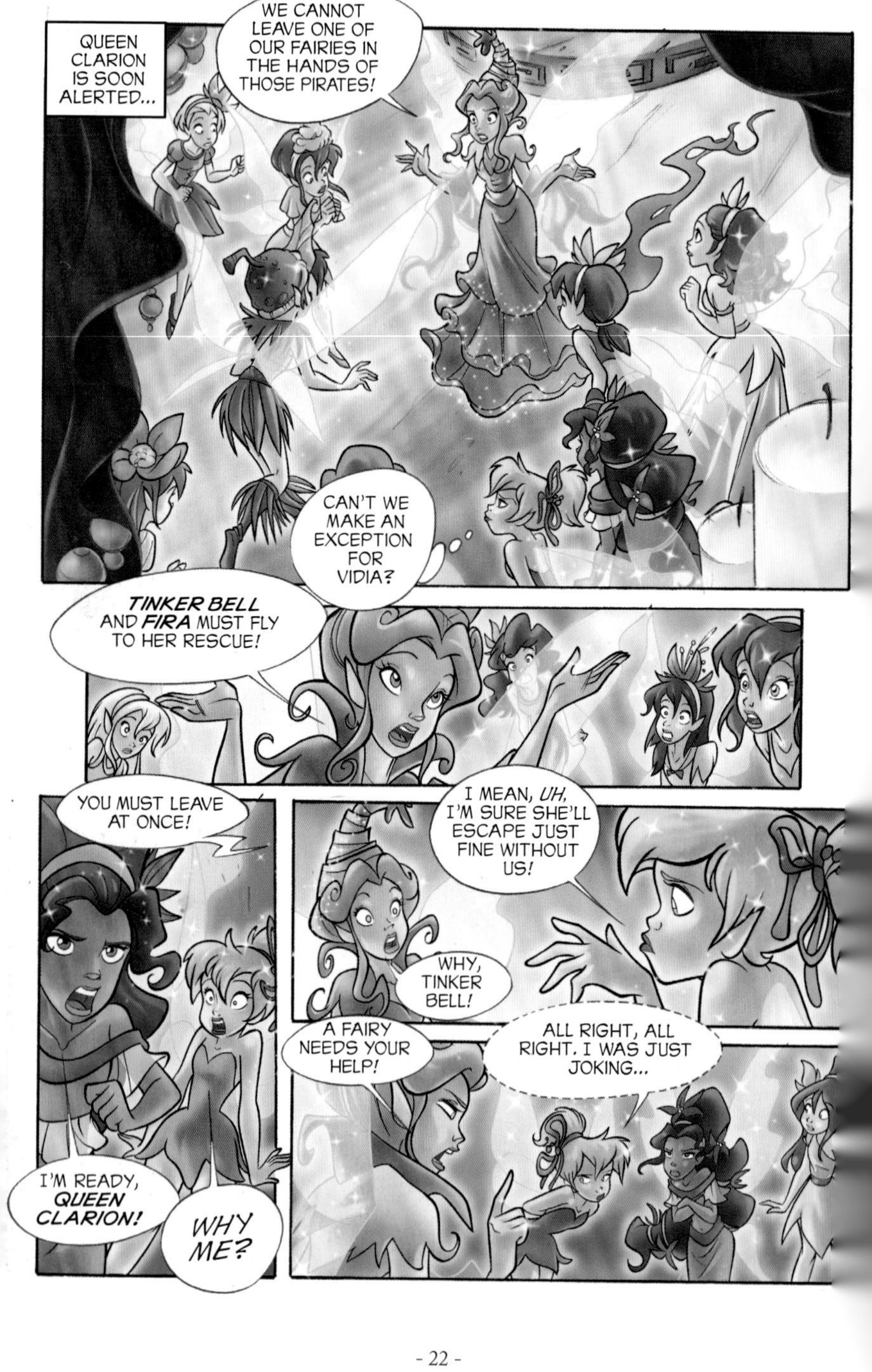
QUEEN CLARION IS SOON ALERTED...
WE CANNOT LEAVE ONE OF OUR FAIRIES IN THE HANDS OF THOSE PIRATES!
CAN'T WE MAKE AN EXCEPTION FOR VIDIA?
TINKER BELL AND FIRA MUST FLY TO HER RESCUE!
YOU MUST LEAVE AT ONCE!
I MEAN, UH, I'M SURE SHE'LL ESCAPE JUST FINE WITHOUT US!
WHY, TINKER BELL!
A FAIRY NEEDS YOUR HELP!
ALL RIGHT, ALL RIGHT. I WAS JUST JOKING...
I'M READY, QUEEN CLARION!
WHY ME?

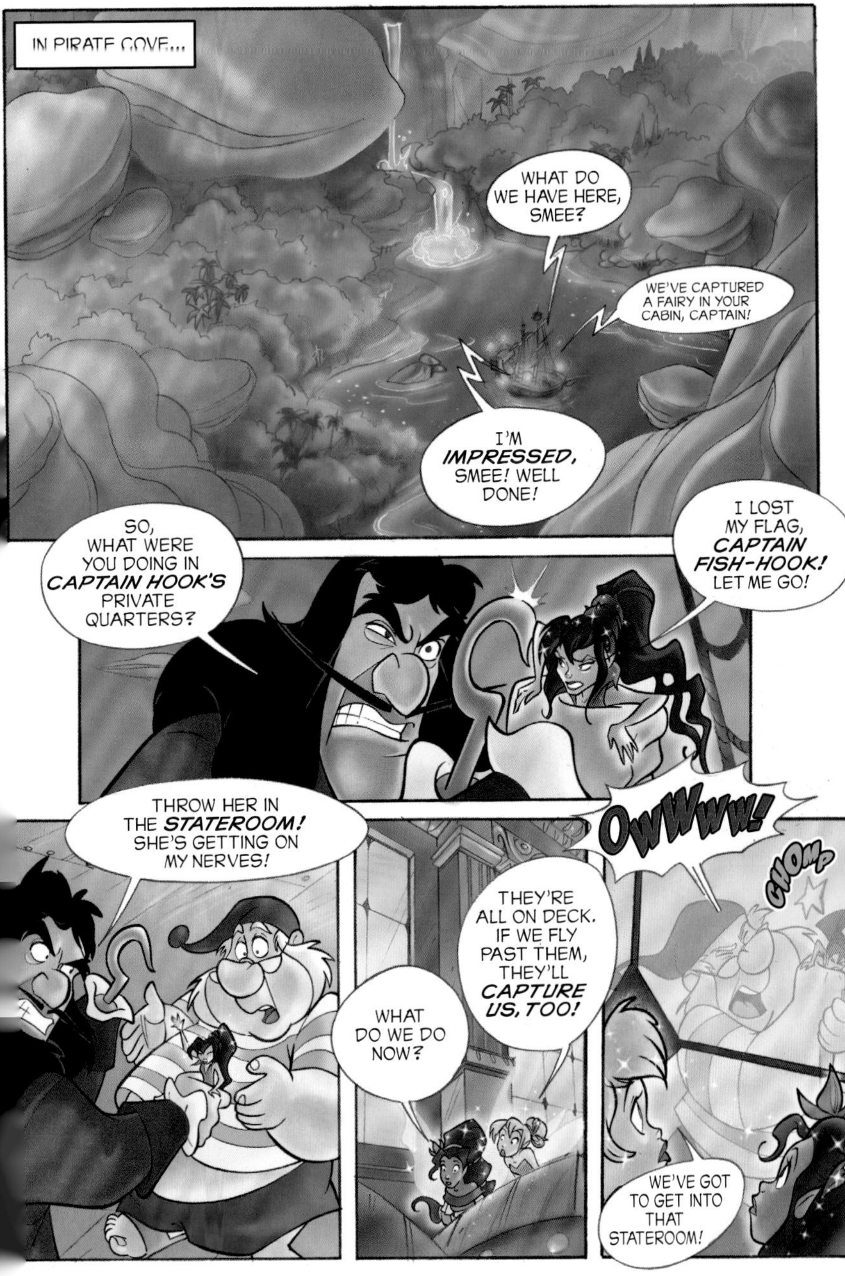
IN PIRATE COVE...
WHAT DO WE HAVE HERE, SMEE?
WE'VE CAPTURED A FAIRY IN YOUR CABIN, CAPTAIN!
I'M IMPRESSED, SMEE! WELL DONE!
SO, WHAT WERE YOU DOING IN CAPTAIN HOOK'S PRIVATE QUARTERS?
I LOST MY FLAG, CAPTAIN FISH-HOOK! LET ME GO!
THROW HER IN THE STATEROOM! SHE'S GETTING ON MY NERVES!
OWWWW!
CHOMP
WHAT DO WE DO NOW?
THEY'RE ALL ON DECK. IF WE FLY PAST THEM, THEY'LL CAPTURE US, TOO!
WE'VE GOT TO GET INTO THAT STATEROOM!

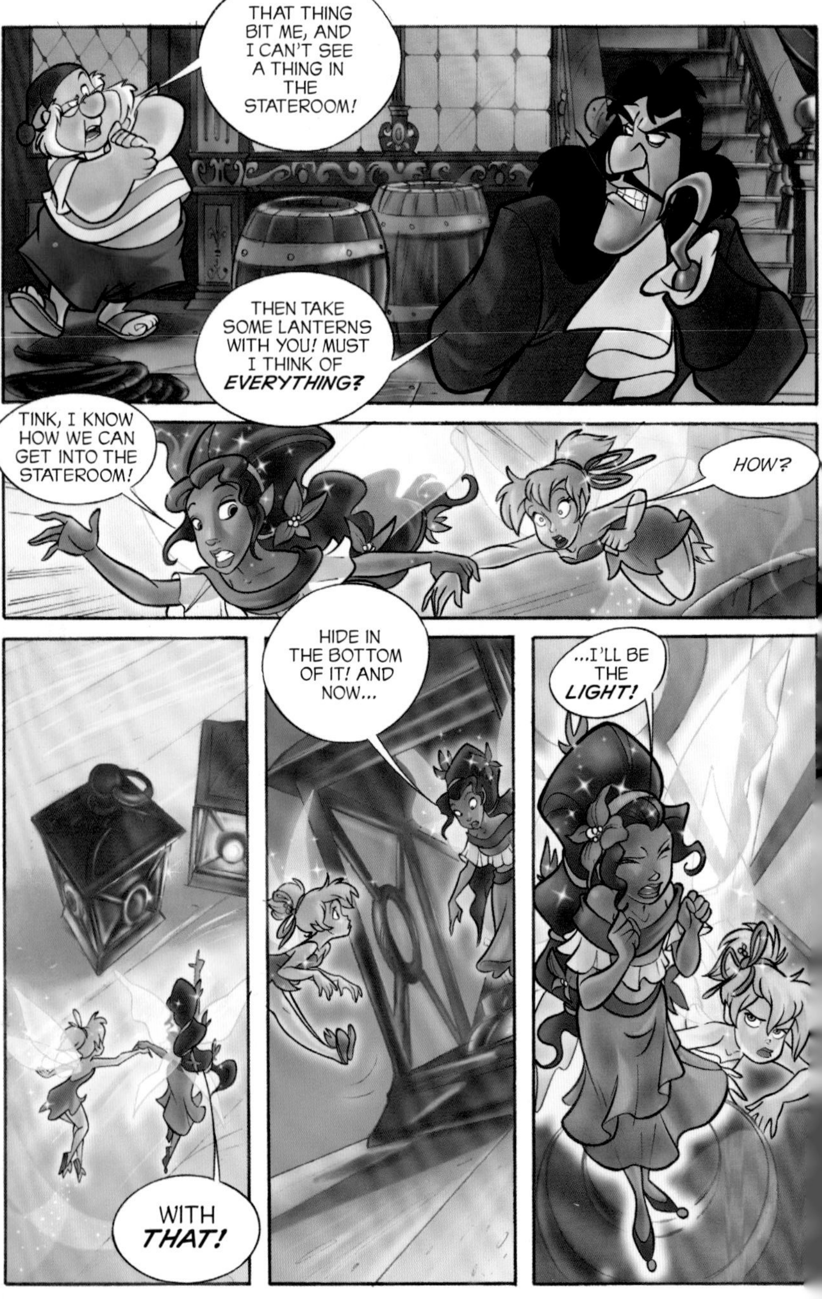
THAT THING BIT ME, AND I CAN'T SEE A THING IN THE STATEROOM!
THEN TAKE SOME LANTERNS WITH YOU! MUST I THINK OF EVERYTHING?
TINK, I KNOW HOW WE CAN GET INTO THE STATEROOM!
HOW?
WITH THAT!
HIDE IN THE BOTTOM OF IT! AND NOW...
...I'LL BE THE LIGHT!

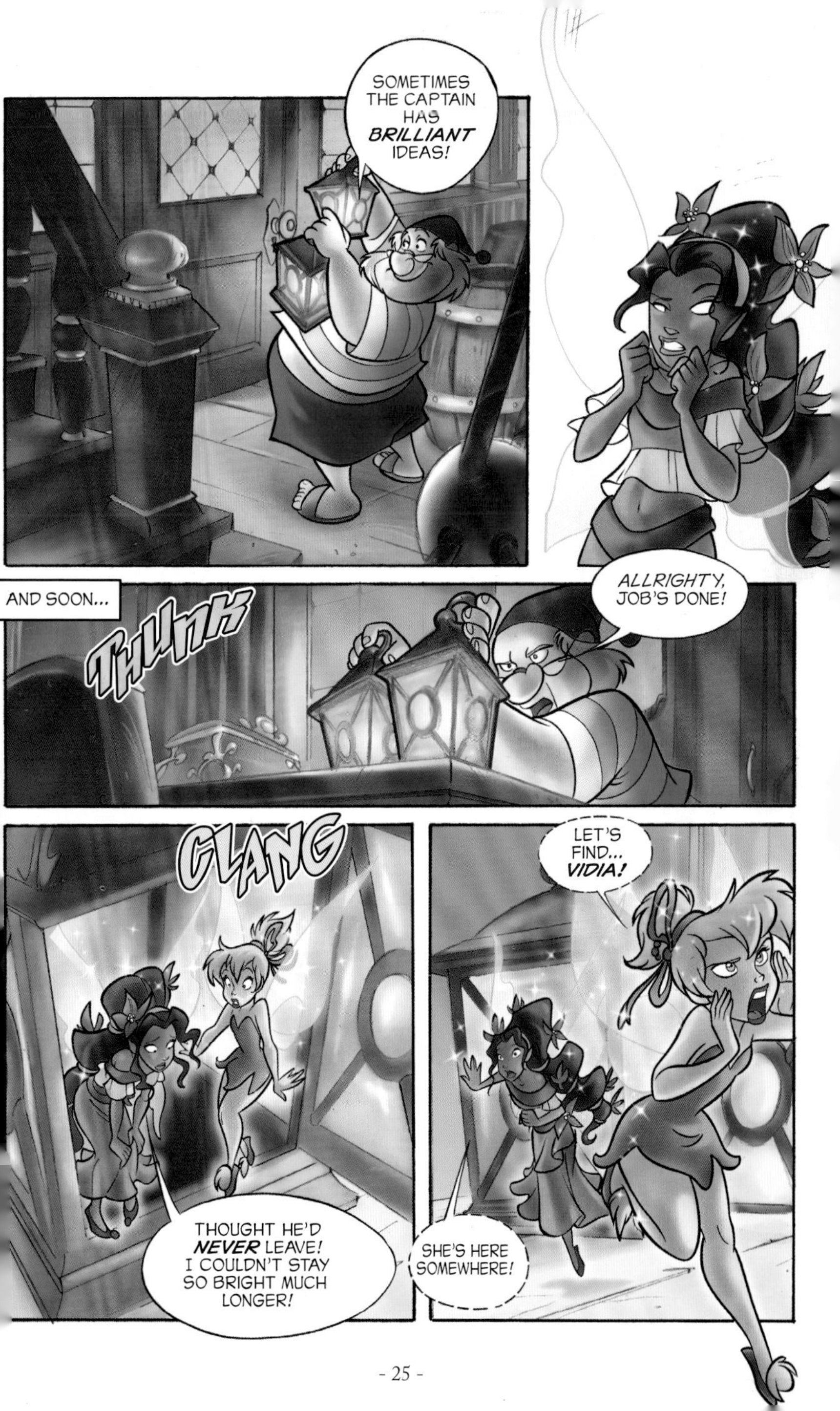
SOMETIMES THE CAPTAIN HAS **BRILLIANT** IDEAS!
AND SOON...
THUNK
ALLRIGHTY, JOB'S DONE!
CLANG
THOUGHT HE'D **NEVER** LEAVE! I COULDN'T STAY SO BRIGHT MUCH LONGER!
LET'S FIND... **VIDIA!**
SHE'S HERE SOMEWHERE!

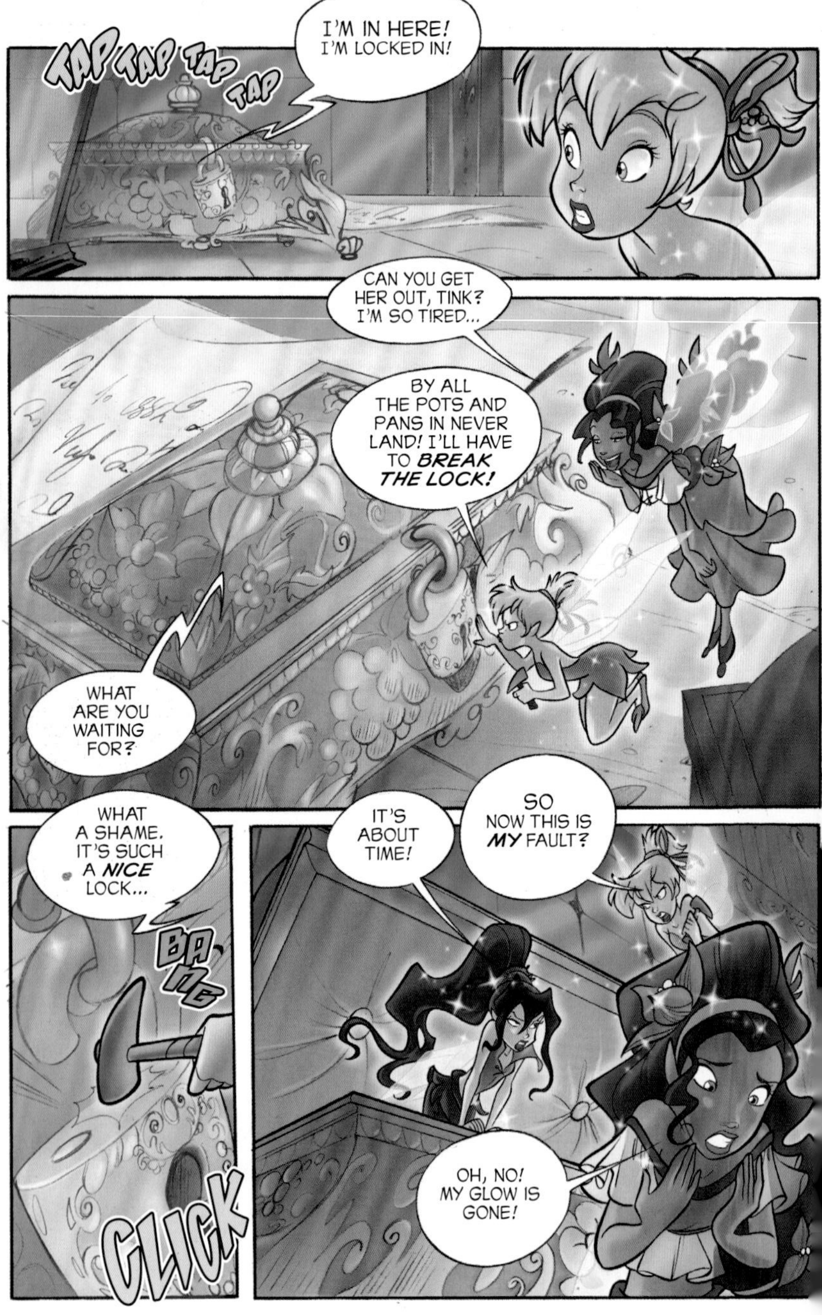
TAP TAP TAP TAP
I'M IN HERE! I'M LOCKED IN!
CAN YOU GET HER OUT, TINK? I'M SO TIRED...
BY ALL THE POTS AND PANS IN NEVER LAND! I'LL HAVE TO BREAK THE LOCK!
WHAT ARE YOU WAITING FOR?
WHAT A SHAME. IT'S SUCH A NICE LOCK...
BANG
CLICK
IT'S ABOUT TIME!
SO NOW THIS IS MY FAULT?
OH, NO! MY GLOW IS GONE!

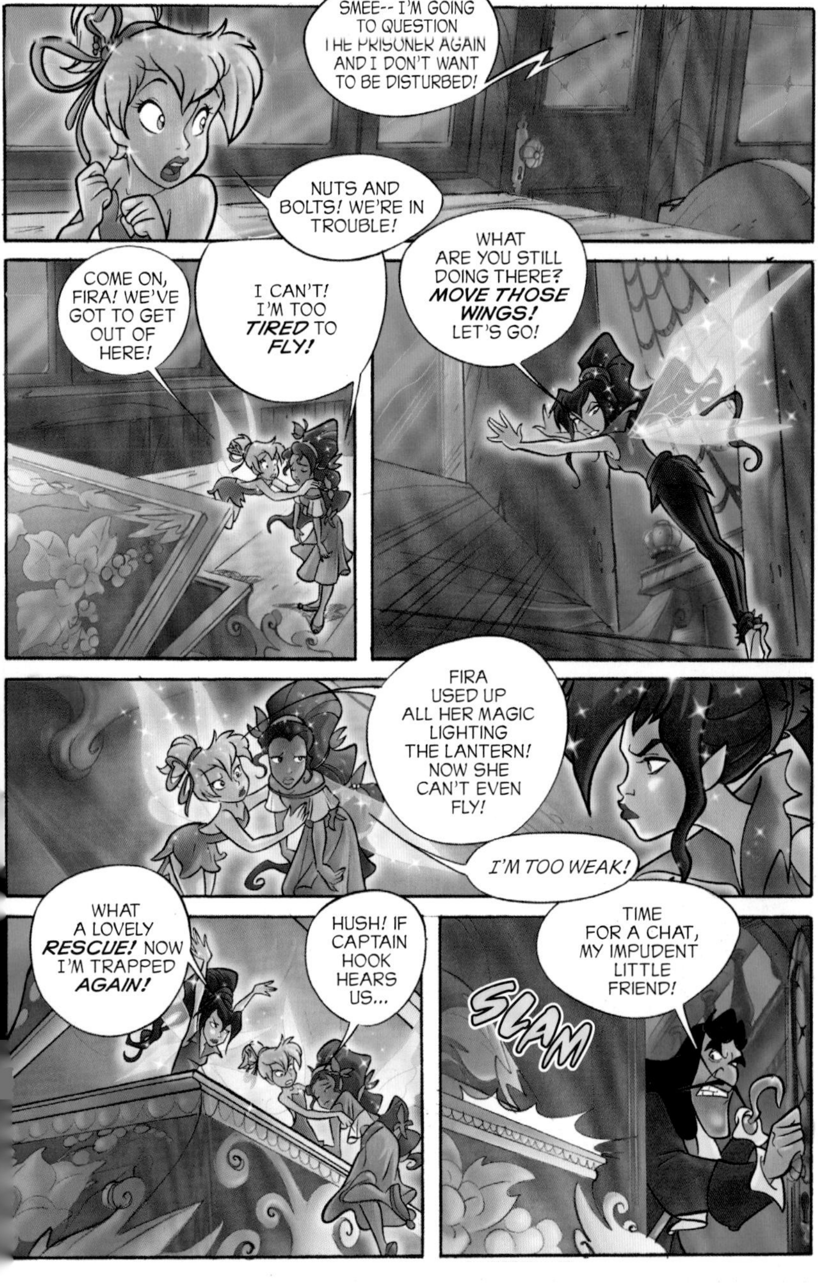
SMEE-- I'M GOING TO QUESTION THE PRISONER AGAIN AND I DON'T WANT TO BE DISTURBED!
NUTS AND BOLTS! WE'RE IN TROUBLE!
COME ON, FIRA! WE'VE GOT TO GET OUT OF HERE!
I CAN'T! I'M TOO TIRED TO FLY!
WHAT ARE YOU STILL DOING THERE? MOVE THOSE WINGS! LET'S GO!
FIRA USED UP ALL HER MAGIC LIGHTING THE LANTERN! NOW SHE CAN'T EVEN FLY!
I'M TOO WEAK!
WHAT A LOVELY RESCUE! NOW I'M TRAPPED AGAIN!
HUSH! IF CAPTAIN HOOK HEARS US...
SLAM
TIME FOR A CHAT, MY IMPUDENT LITTLE FRIEND!

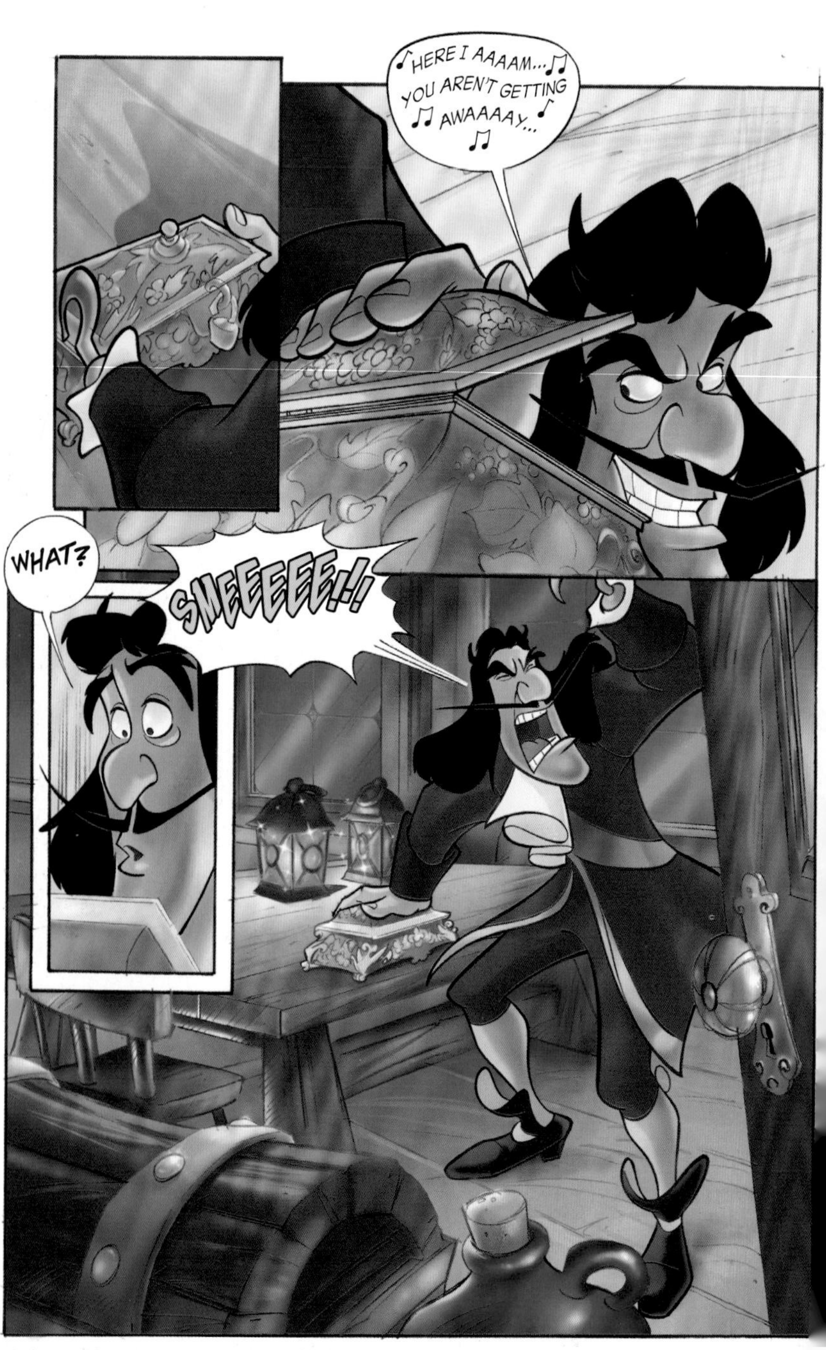

♪HERE I AAAAM...♫ YOU AREN'T GETTING ♫ AWAAAAY...♪ ♫
WHAT?
SMEEEEE!!!

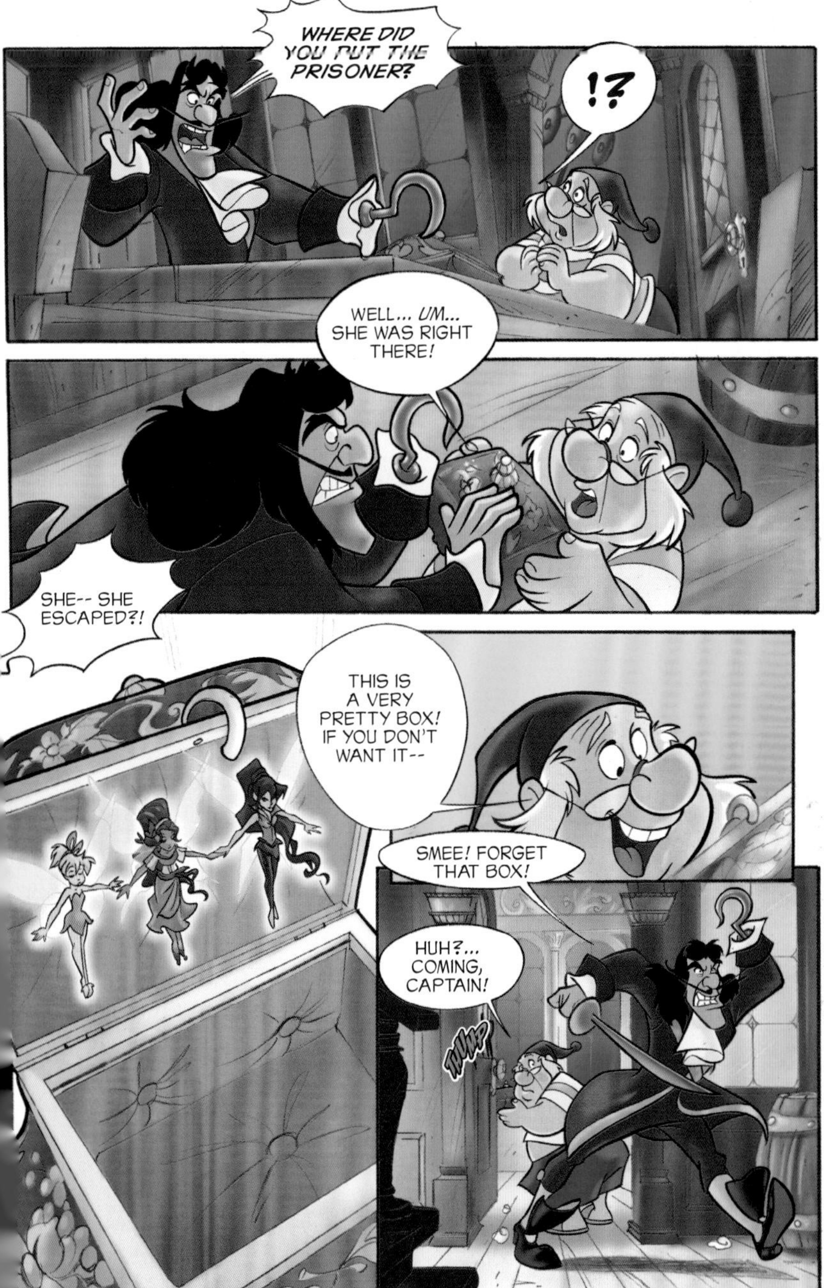
WHERE DID YOU PUT THE PRISONER?
!?
WELL... UM... SHE WAS RIGHT THERE!
SHE-- SHE ESCAPED?!
THIS IS A VERY PRETTY BOX! IF YOU DON'T WANT IT--
SMEE! FORGET THAT BOX!
HUH?... COMING, CAPTAIN!
THUMP

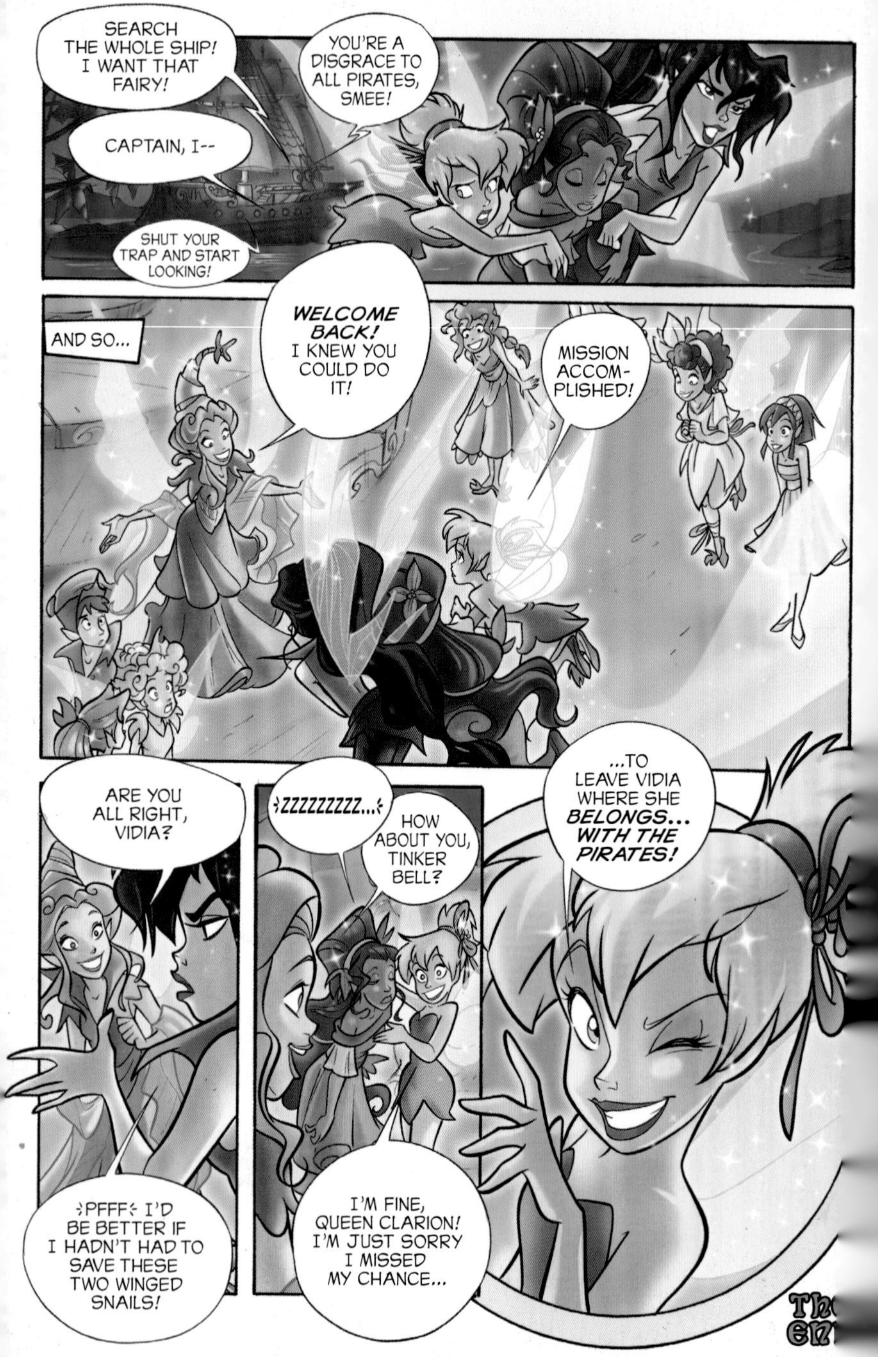
SEARCH THE WHOLE SHIP! I WANT THAT FAIRY!
YOU'RE A DISGRACE TO ALL PIRATES, SMEE!
CAPTAIN, I--
SHUT YOUR TRAP AND START LOOKING!
AND SO...
WELCOME BACK! I KNEW YOU COULD DO IT!
MISSION ACCOM-PLISHED!
ARE YOU ALL RIGHT, VIDIA?
PFFF I'D BE BETTER IF I HADN'T HAD TO SAVE THESE TWO WINGED SNAILS!
ZZZZZZZZZ...
HOW ABOUT YOU, TINKER BELL?
I'M FINE, QUEEN CLARION! I'M JUST SORRY I MISSED MY CHANCE...
...TO LEAVE VIDIA WHERE SHE BELONGS... WITH THE PIRATES!

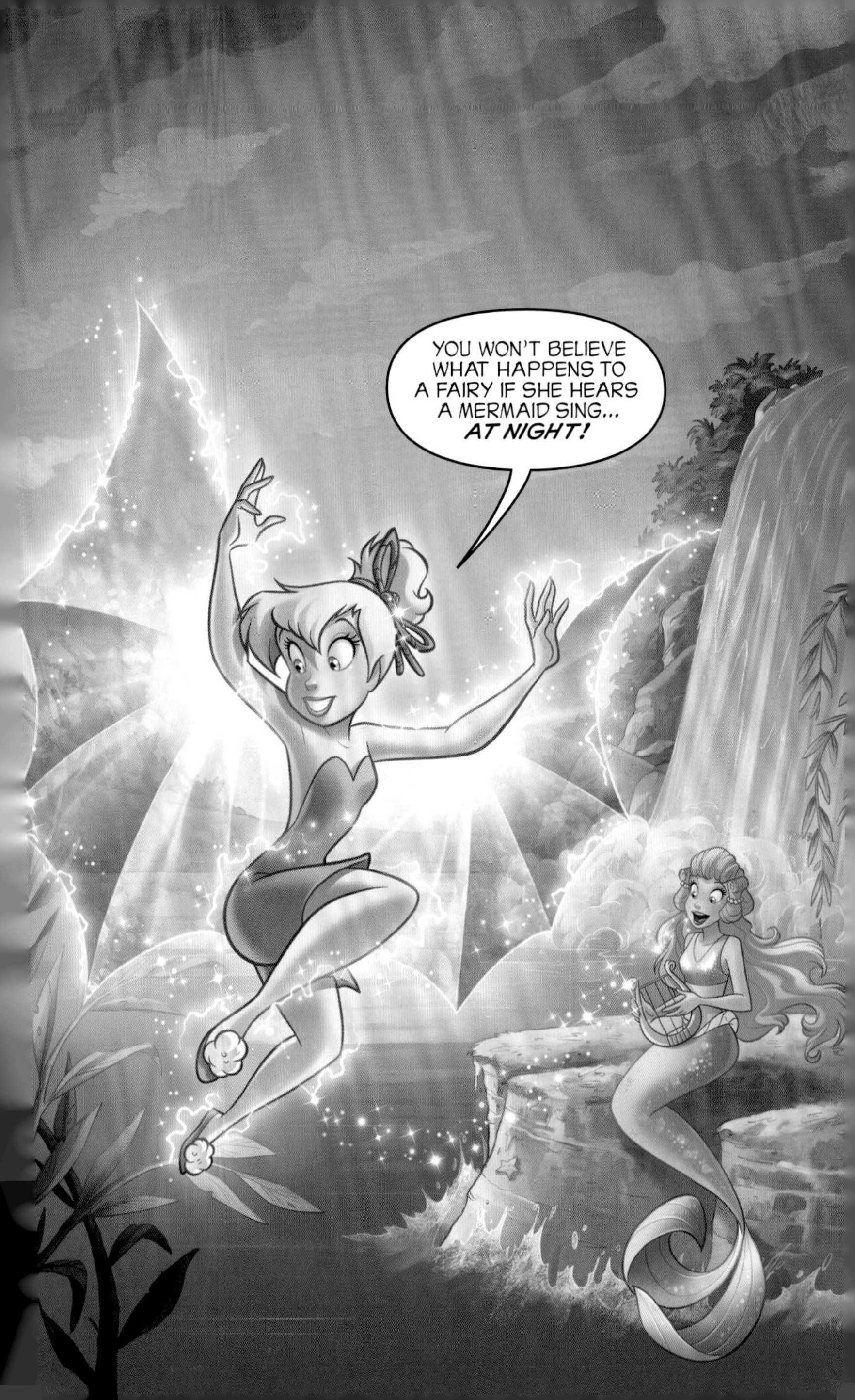
YOU WON'T BELIEVE WHAT HAPPENS TO A FAIRY IF SHE HEARS A MERMAID SING... AT NIGHT!

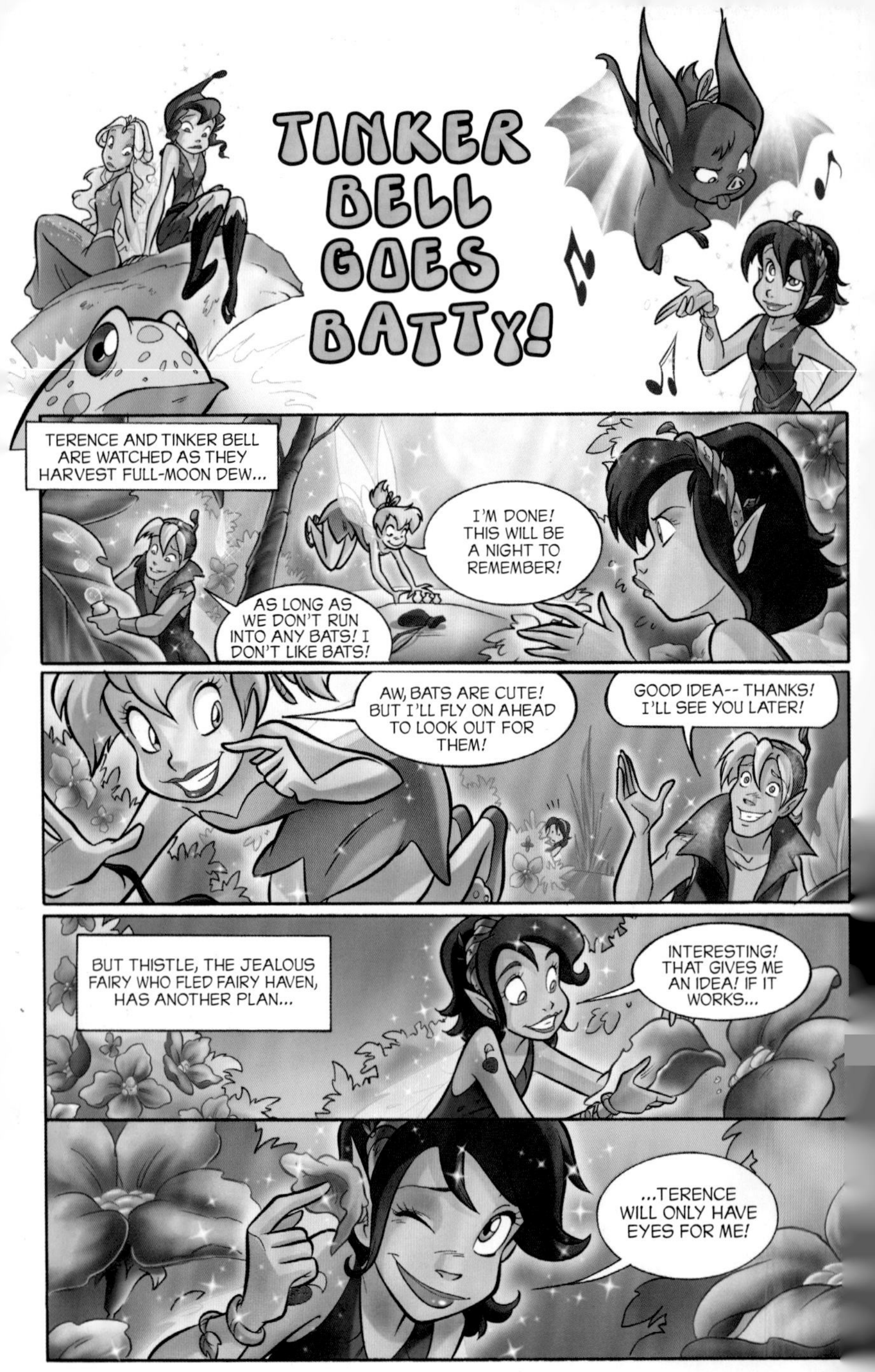
TINKER BELL GOES BATTY!
TERENCE AND TINKER BELL ARE WATCHED AS THEY HARVEST FULL-MOON DEW...
I'M DONE! THIS WILL BE A NIGHT TO REMEMBER!
AS LONG AS WE DON'T RUN INTO ANY BATS! I DON'T LIKE BATS!
AW, BATS ARE CUTE! BUT I'LL FLY ON AHEAD TO LOOK OUT FOR THEM!
GOOD IDEA-- THANKS! I'LL SEE YOU LATER!
BUT THISTLE, THE JEALOUS FAIRY WHO FLED FAIRY HAVEN, HAS ANOTHER PLAN...
INTERESTING! THAT GIVES ME AN IDEA! IF IT WORKS...
...TERENCE WILL ONLY HAVE EYES FOR ME!

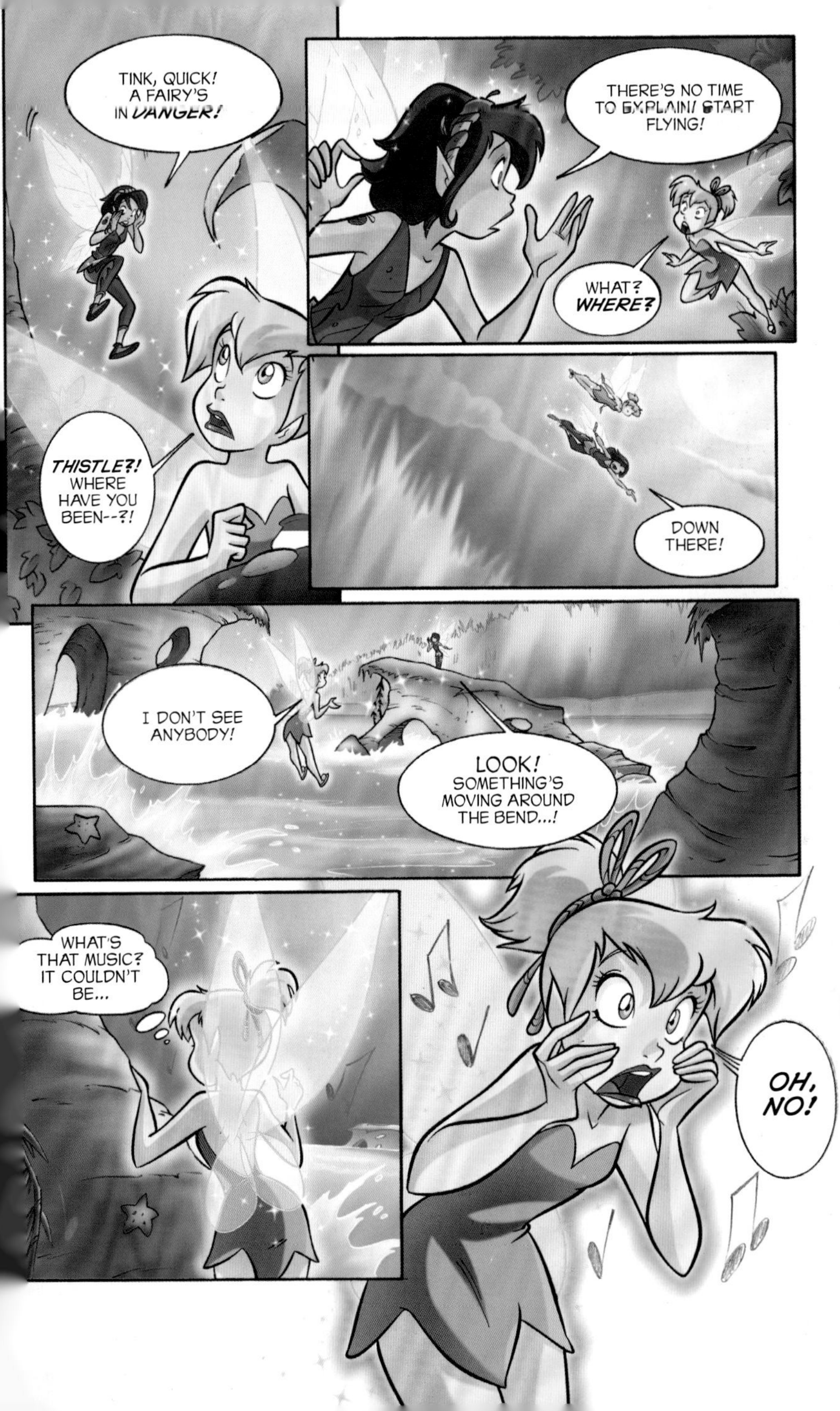
TINK, QUICK! A FAIRY'S IN DANGER!
THISTLE?! WHERE HAVE YOU BEEN--?!
THERE'S NO TIME TO EXPLAIN! START FLYING!
WHAT? WHERE?
DOWN THERE!
I DON'T SEE ANYBODY!
LOOK! SOMETHING'S MOVING AROUND THE BEND...!
WHAT'S THAT MUSIC? IT COULDN'T BE...
OH, NO!

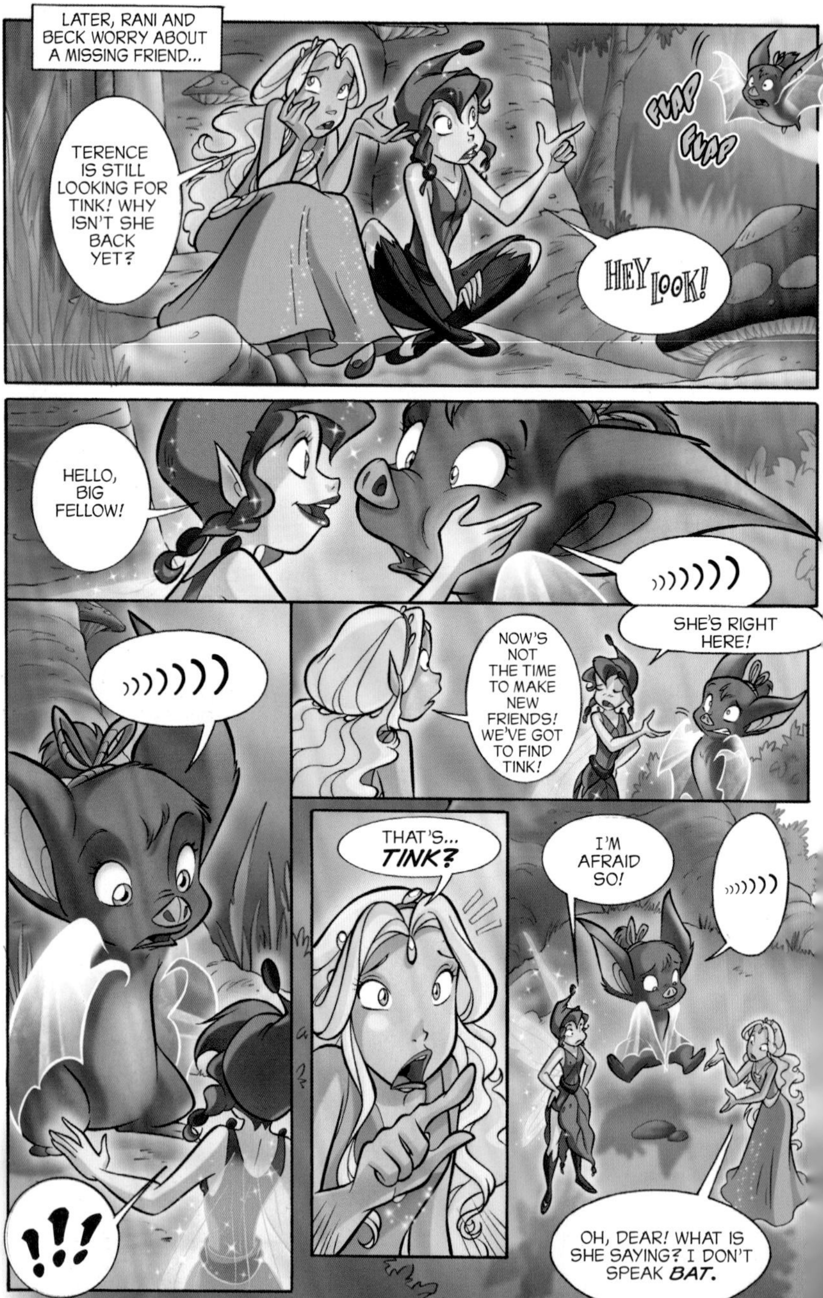
LATER, RANI AND BECK WORRY ABOUT A MISSING FRIEND...
TERENCE IS STILL LOOKING FOR TINK! WHY ISN'T SHE BACK YET?
FLAP FLAP
HEY LOOK!
HELLO, BIG FELLOW!
NOW'S NOT THE TIME TO MAKE NEW FRIENDS! WE'VE GOT TO FIND TINK!
SHE'S RIGHT HERE!
!!!
THAT'S... TINK?
I'M AFRAID SO!
OH, DEAR! WHAT IS SHE SAYING? I DON'T SPEAK BAT.

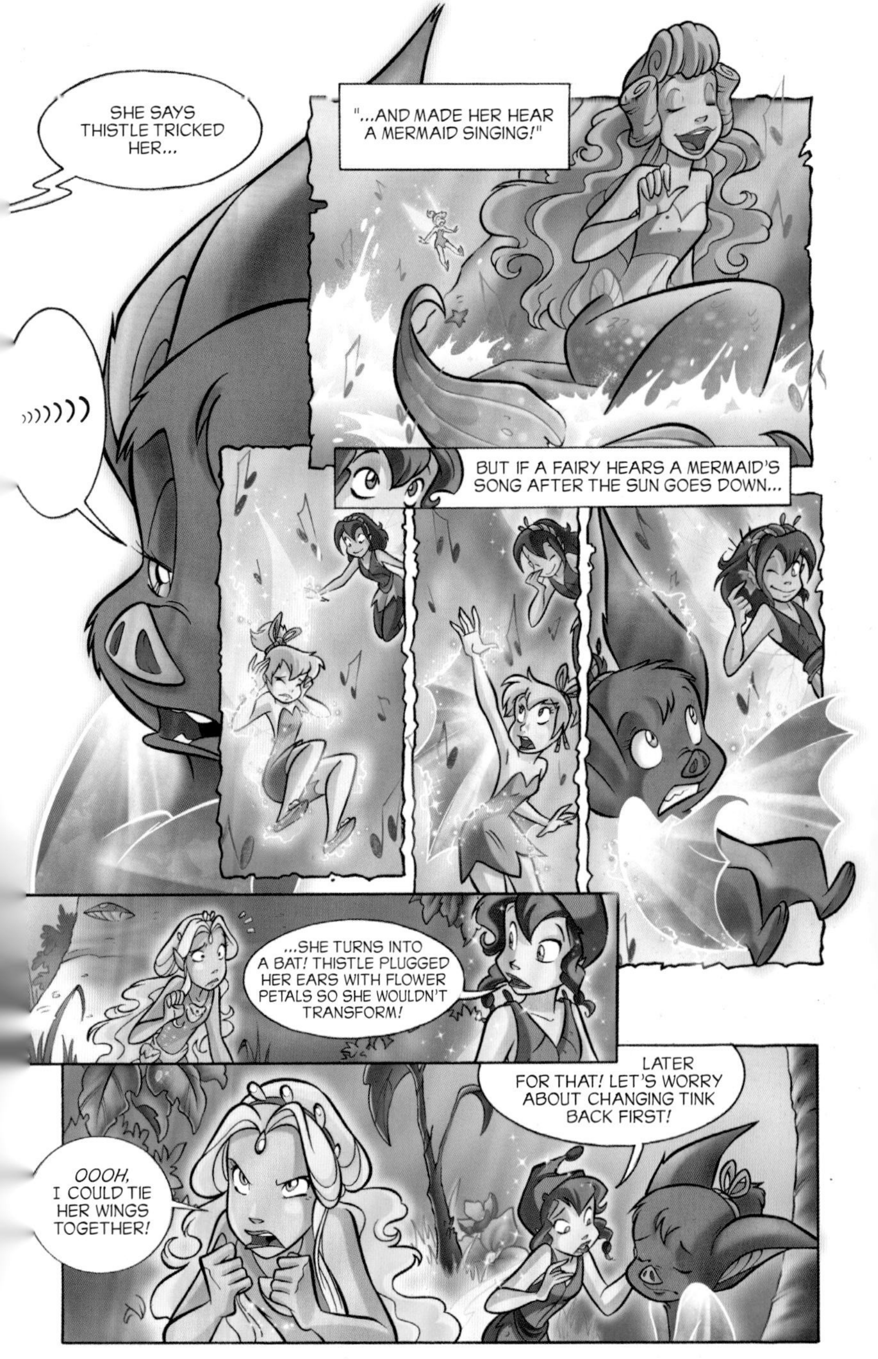
SHE SAYS THISTLE TRICKED HER...
"...AND MADE HER HEAR A MERMAID SINGING!"
BUT IF A FAIRY HEARS A MERMAID'S SONG AFTER THE SUN GOES DOWN...
...SHE TURNS INTO A BAT! THISTLE PLUGGED HER EARS WITH FLOWER PETALS SO SHE WOULDN'T TRANSFORM!
OOOH, I COULD TIE HER WINGS TOGETHER!
LATER FOR THAT! LET'S WORRY ABOUT CHANGING TINK BACK FIRST!

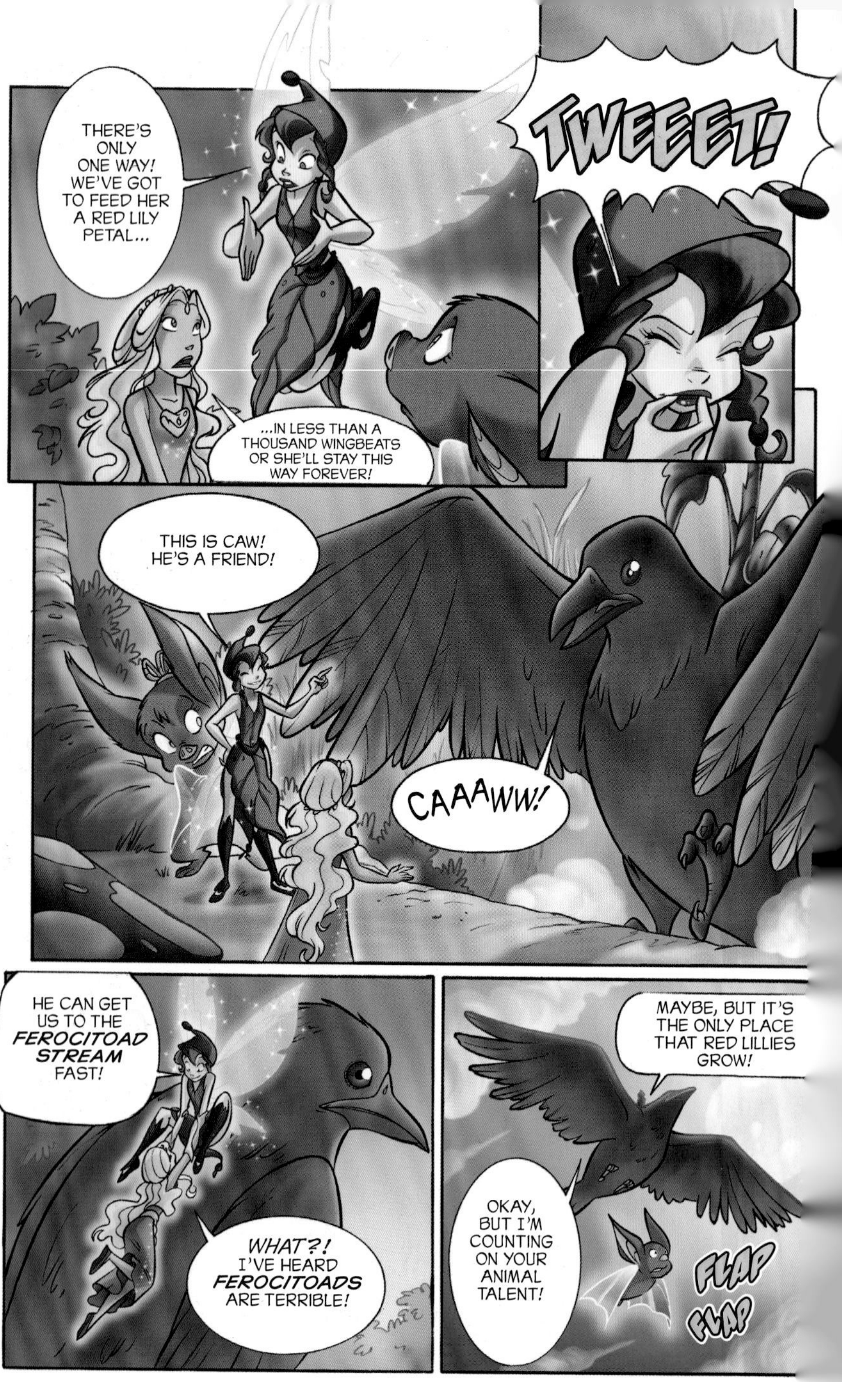
THERE'S ONLY ONE WAY! WE'VE GOT TO FEED HER A RED LILY PETAL...
TWEEET!
...IN LESS THAN A THOUSAND WINGBEATS OR SHE'LL STAY THIS WAY FOREVER!
THIS IS CAW! HE'S A FRIEND!
CAAAWW!
HE CAN GET US TO THE *FEROCITOAD STREAM* FAST!
WHAT?! I'VE HEARD *FEROCITOADS* ARE TERRIBLE!
MAYBE, BUT IT'S THE ONLY PLACE THAT RED LILLIES GROW!
OKAY, BUT I'M COUNTING ON YOUR ANIMAL TALENT!
FLAP
FLAP

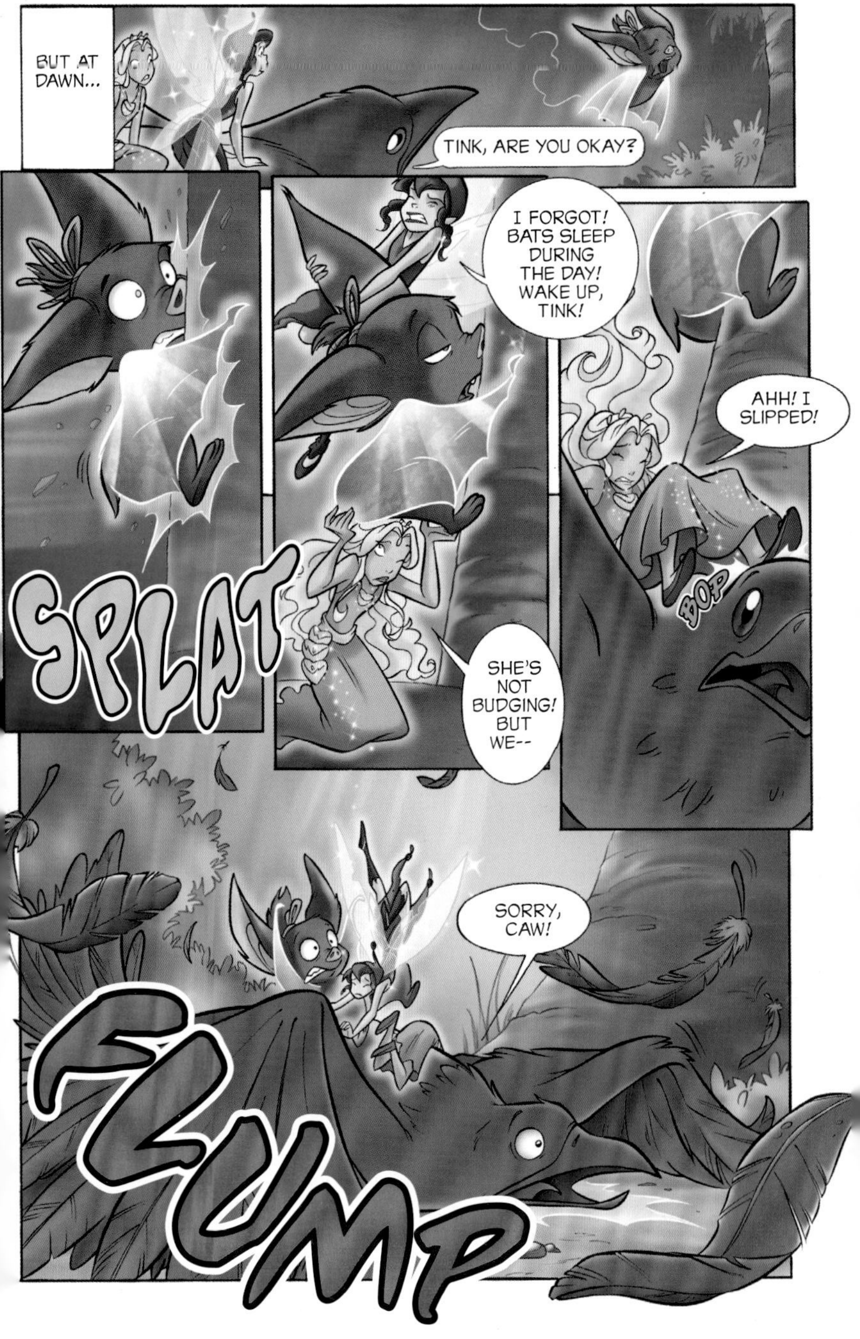
BUT AT DAWN...
TINK, ARE YOU OKAY?
I FORGOT! BATS SLEEP DURING THE DAY! WAKE UP, TINK!
AHH! I SLIPPED!
SPLAT
SHE'S NOT BUDGING! BUT WE--
BOP
SORRY, CAW!
FLUMP

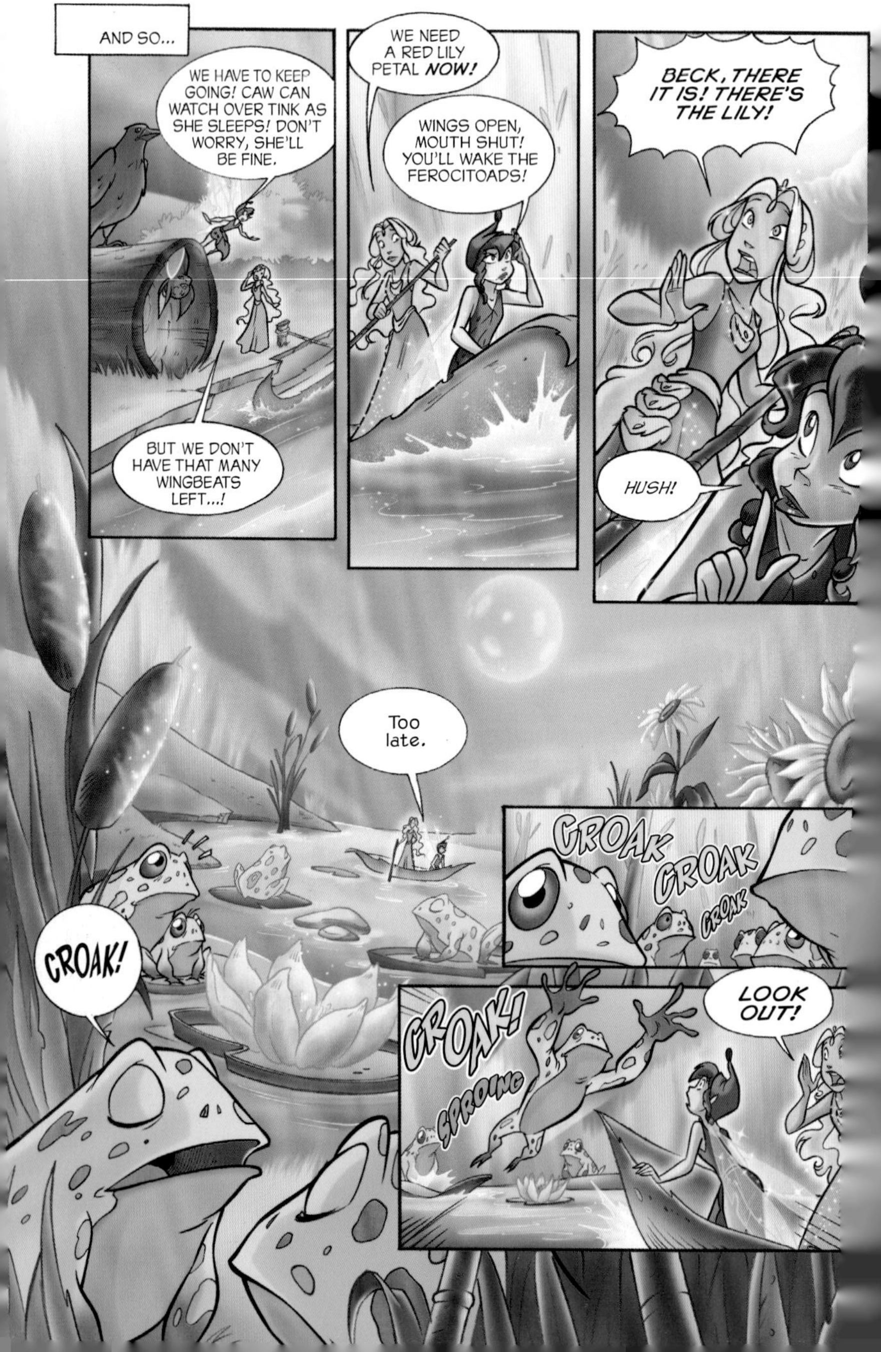
AND SO...
WE HAVE TO KEEP GOING! CAW CAN WATCH OVER TINK AS SHE SLEEPS! DON'T WORRY, SHE'LL BE FINE.
BUT WE DON'T HAVE THAT MANY WINGBEATS LEFT...!
WE NEED A RED LILY PETAL NOW!
WINGS OPEN, MOUTH SHUT! YOU'LL WAKE THE FEROCITOADS!
BECK, THERE IT IS! THERE'S THE LILY!
HUSH!
Too late.
CROAK!
CROAK
CROAK
CROAK
CROAK!
SPROING
LOOK OUT!

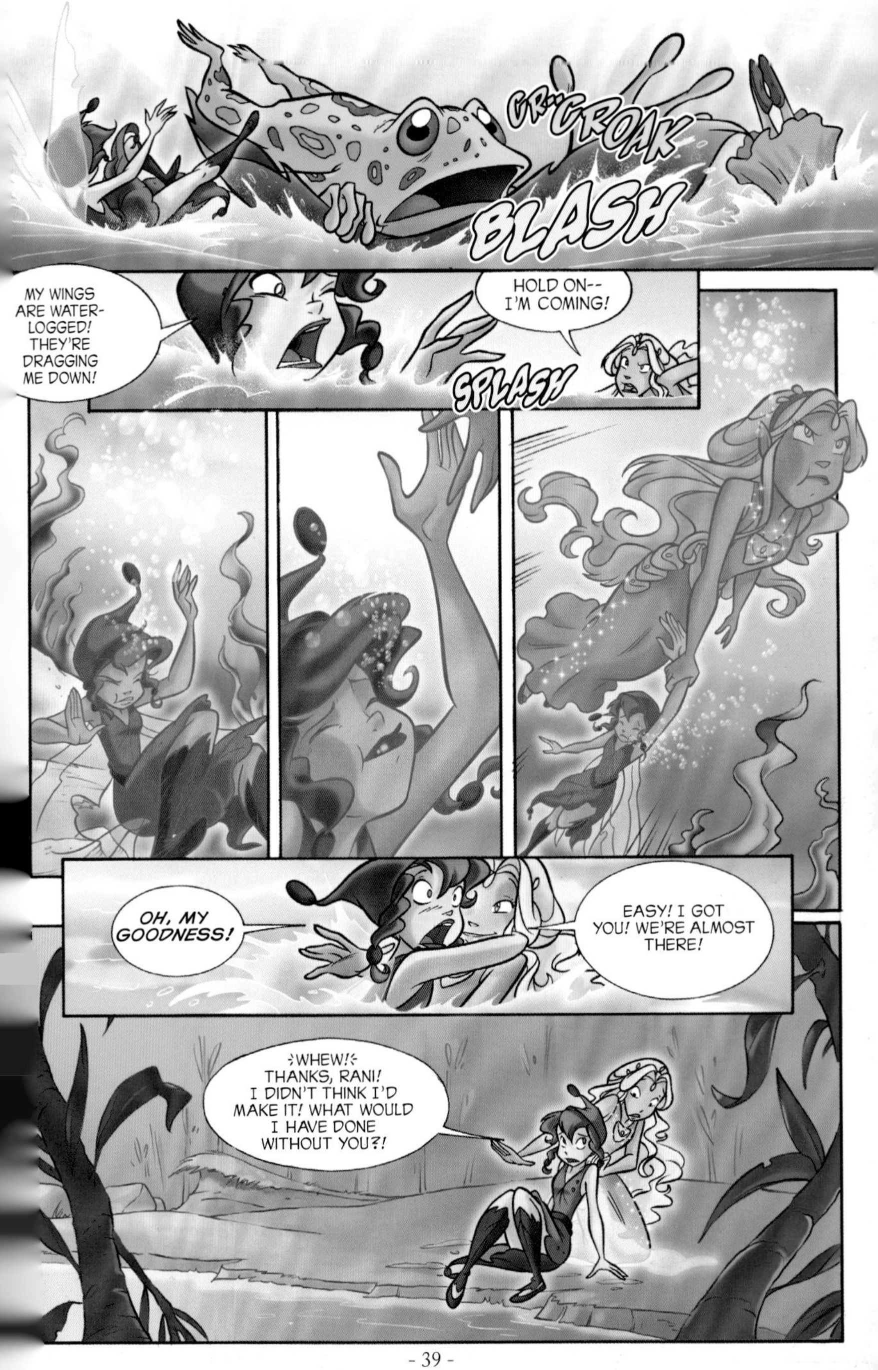
CR-CROAK
BLASH
MY WINGS ARE WATER-LOGGED! THEY'RE DRAGGING ME DOWN!
HOLD ON-- I'M COMING!
SPLASH
OH, MY GOODNESS!
EASY! I GOT YOU! WE'RE ALMOST THERE!
WHEW! THANKS, RANI! I DIDN'T THINK I'D MAKE IT! WHAT WOULD I HAVE DONE WITHOUT YOU?!

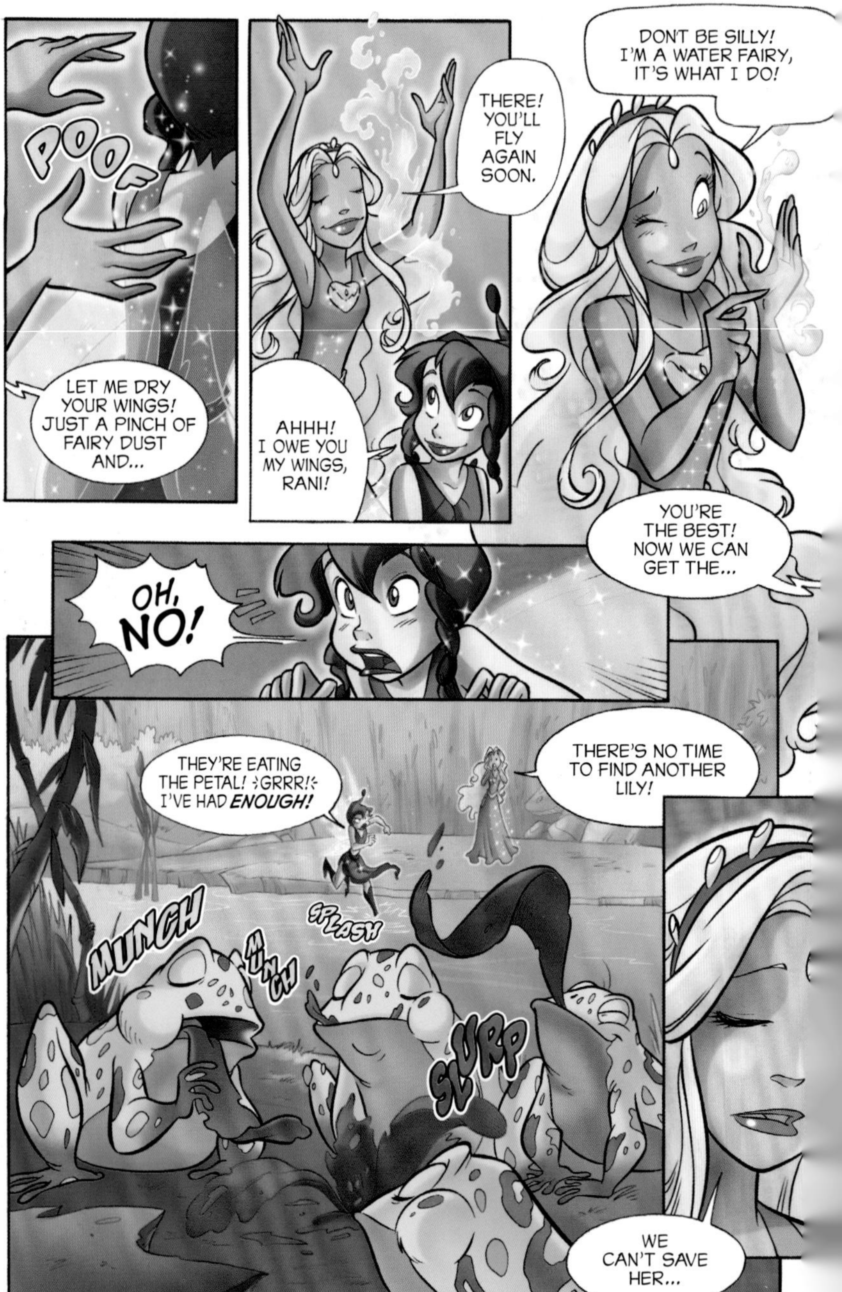
POOF
LET ME DRY YOUR WINGS! JUST A PINCH OF FAIRY DUST AND...
THERE! YOU'LL FLY AGAIN SOON.
AHHH! I OWE YOU MY WINGS, RANI!
DON'T BE SILLY! I'M A WATER FAIRY, IT'S WHAT I DO!
YOU'RE THE BEST! NOW WE CAN GET THE...
OH, NO!
THEY'RE EATING THE PETAL! GRRR! I'VE HAD ENOUGH!
THERE'S NO TIME TO FIND ANOTHER LILY!
MUNCH
MUNCH
SPLASH
SLURP
WE CAN'T SAVE HER...

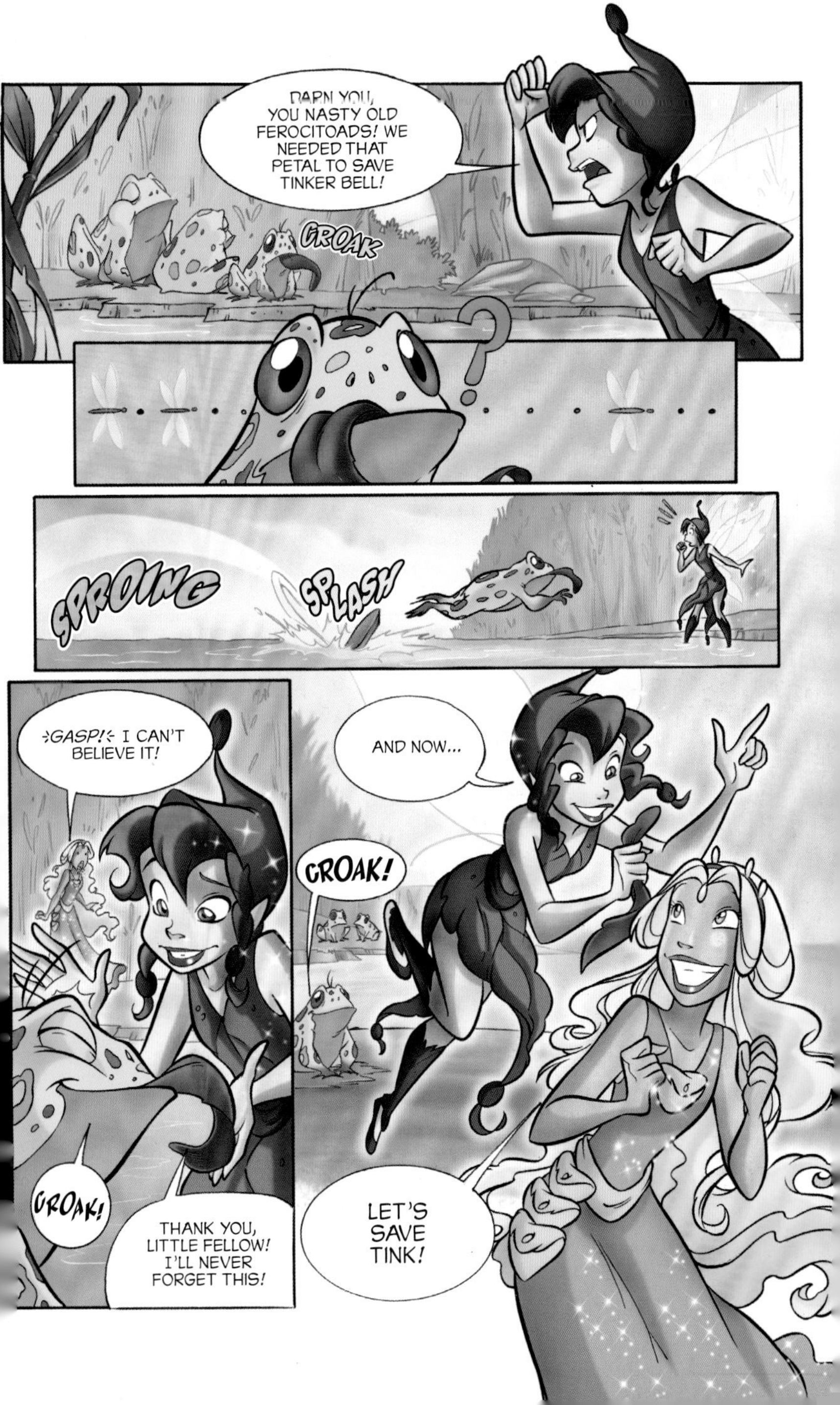
DARN YOU, YOU NASTY OLD FEROCITOADS! WE NEEDED THAT PETAL TO SAVE TINKER BELL!
CROAK
SPROING
SPLASH
GASP! I CAN'T BELIEVE IT!
AND NOW...
CROAK!
CROAK!
THANK YOU, LITTLE FELLOW! I'LL NEVER FORGET THIS!
LET'S SAVE TINK!

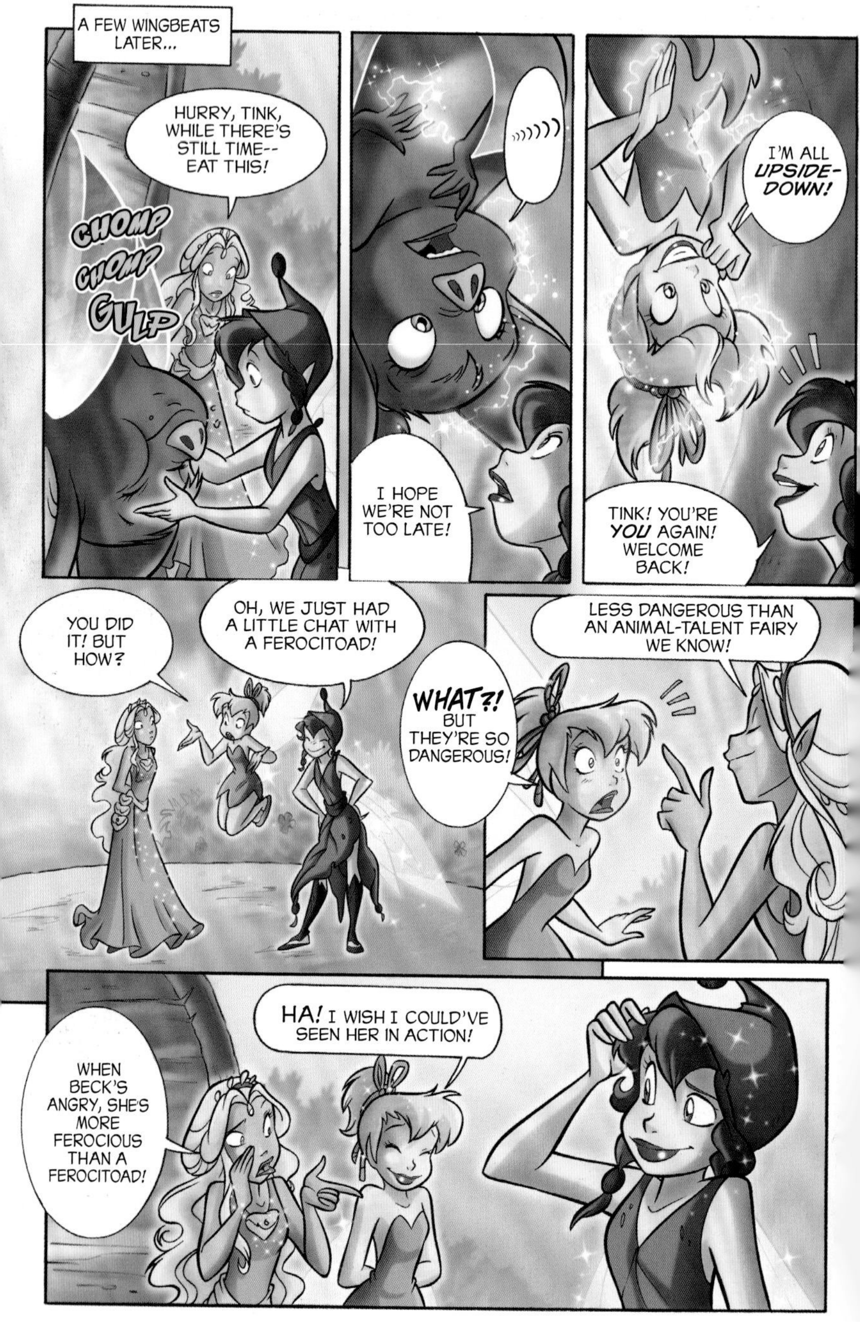
A FEW WINGBEATS LATER...
HURRY, TINK, WHILE THERE'S STILL TIME-- EAT THIS!
CHOMP
CHOMP
GULP
I HOPE WE'RE NOT TOO LATE!
I'M ALL UPSIDE-DOWN!
TINK! YOU'RE YOU AGAIN! WELCOME BACK!
YOU DID IT! BUT HOW?
OH, WE JUST HAD A LITTLE CHAT WITH A FEROCITOAD!
LESS DANGEROUS THAN AN ANIMAL-TALENT FAIRY WE KNOW!
WHAT?! BUT THEY'RE SO DANGEROUS!
HA! I WISH I COULD'VE SEEN HER IN ACTION!
WHEN BECK'S ANGRY, SHE'S MORE FEROCIOUS THAN A FEROCITOAD!

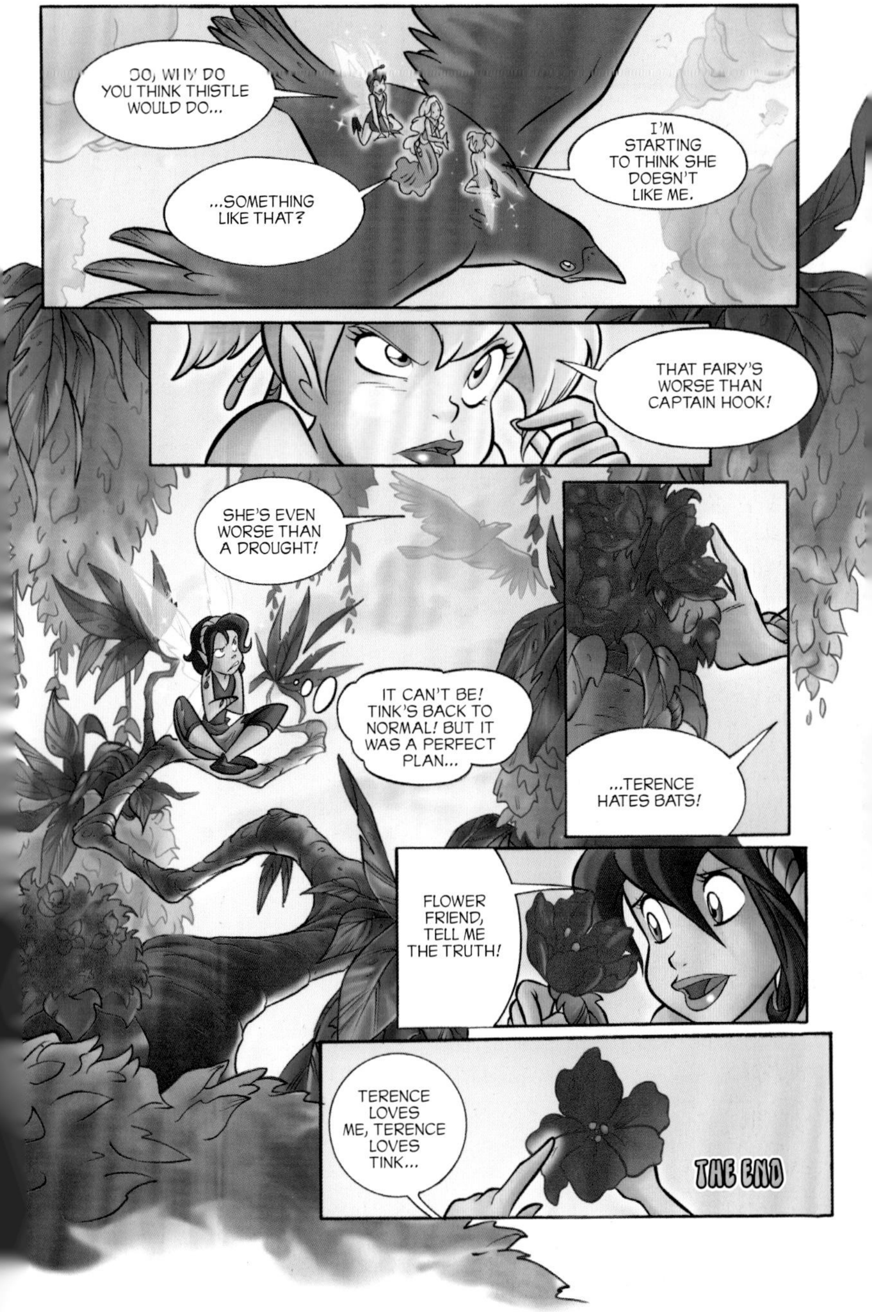
SO, WHY DO YOU THINK THISTLE WOULD DO...
...SOMETHING LIKE THAT?
I'M STARTING TO THINK SHE DOESN'T LIKE ME.
THAT FAIRY'S WORSE THAN CAPTAIN HOOK!
SHE'S EVEN WORSE THAN A DROUGHT!
IT CAN'T BE! TINK'S BACK TO NORMAL! BUT IT WAS A PERFECT PLAN...
...TERENCE HATES BATS!
FLOWER FRIEND, TELL ME THE TRUTH!
TERENCE LOVES ME, TERENCE LOVES TINK...
THE END

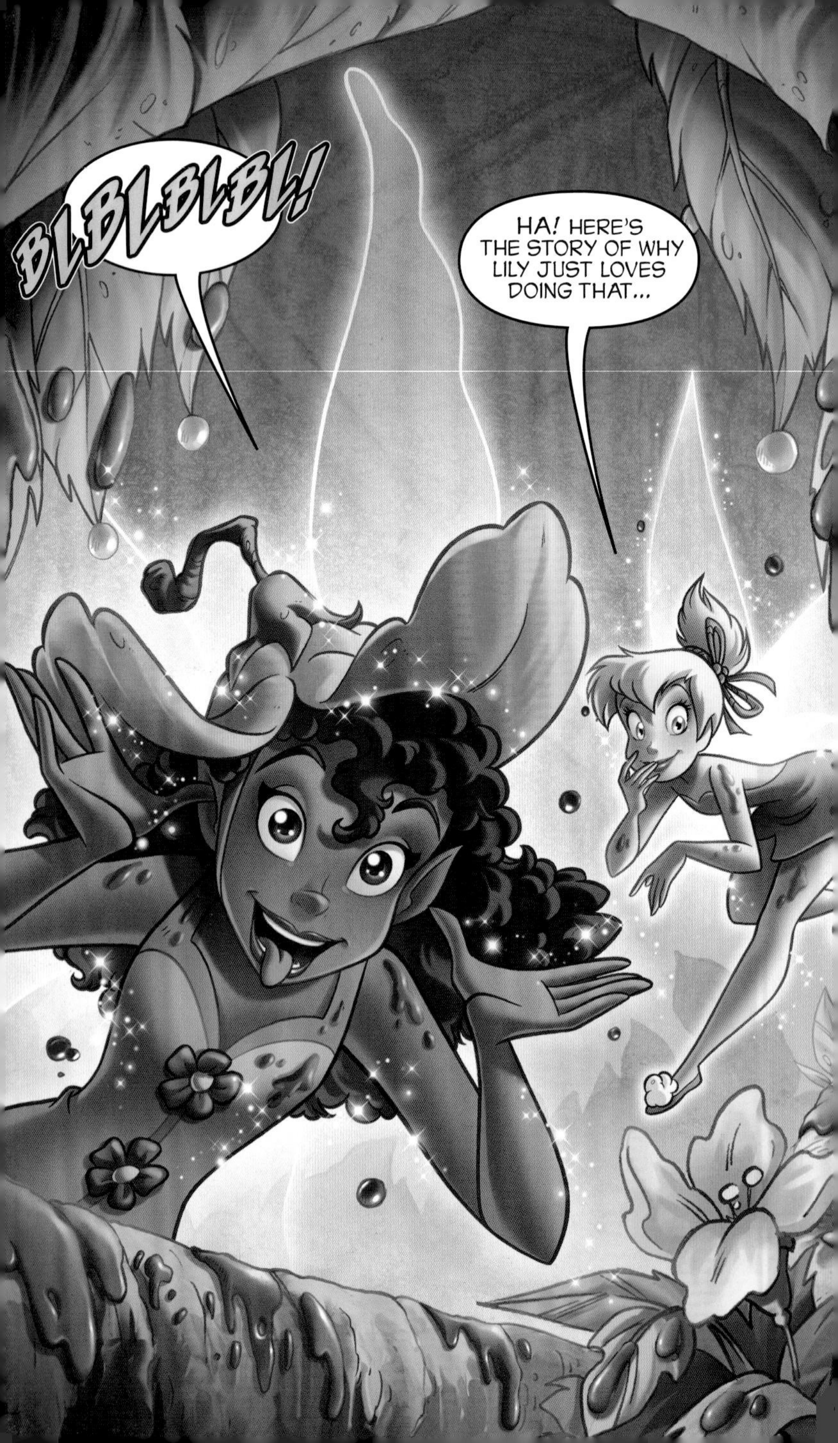
BLBLBLBL!
HA! HERE'S THE STORY OF WHY LILY JUST LOVES DOING THAT...

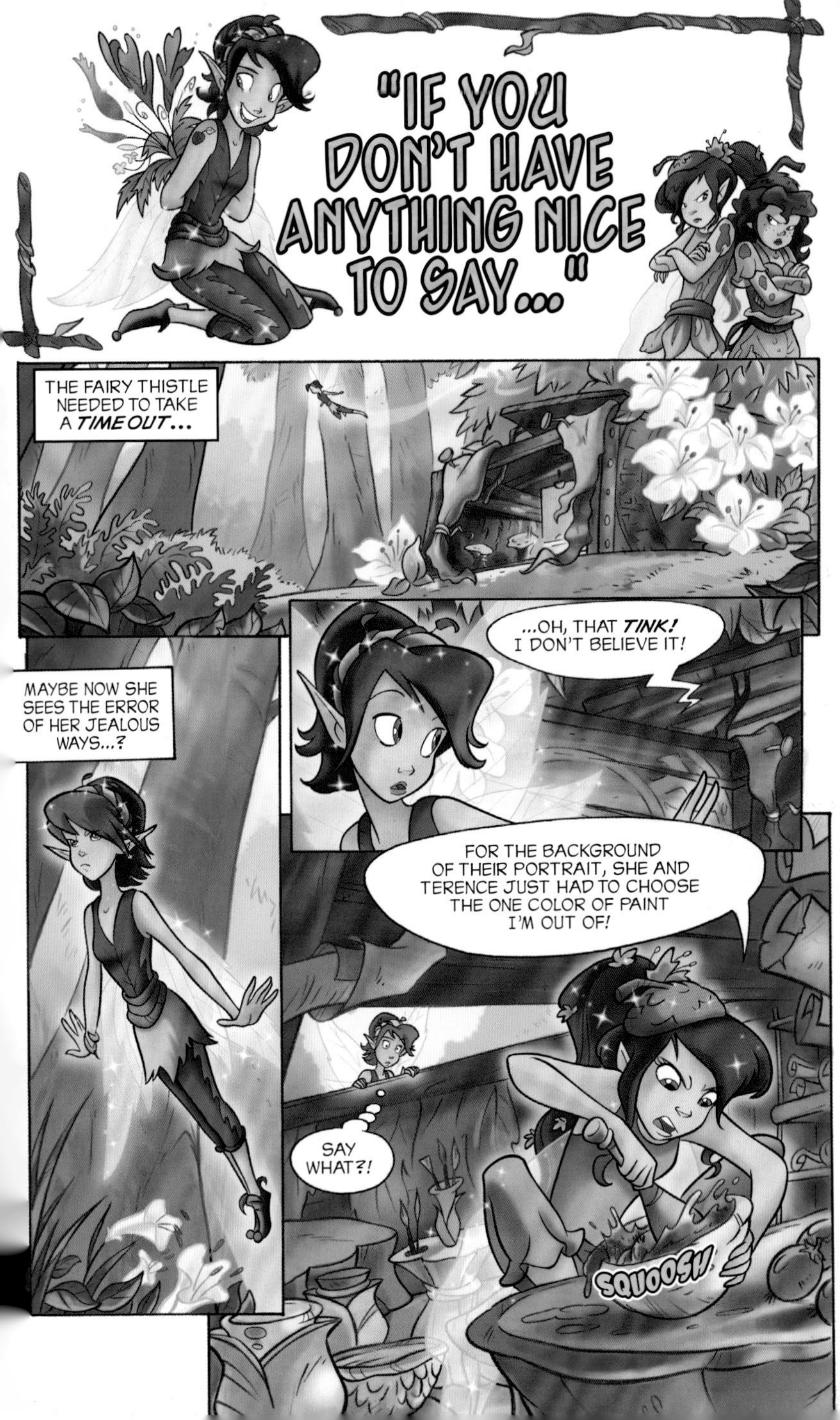
"IF YOU DON'T HAVE ANYTHING NICE TO SAY..."
THE FAIRY THISTLE NEEDED TO TAKE A *TIME OUT*...
...OH, THAT *TINK!* I DON'T BELIEVE IT!
MAYBE NOW SHE SEES THE ERROR OF HER JEALOUS WAYS...?
FOR THE BACKGROUND OF THEIR PORTRAIT, SHE AND TERENCE JUST HAD TO CHOOSE THE ONE COLOR OF PAINT I'M OUT OF!
SAY WHAT?!
SQUOOSH

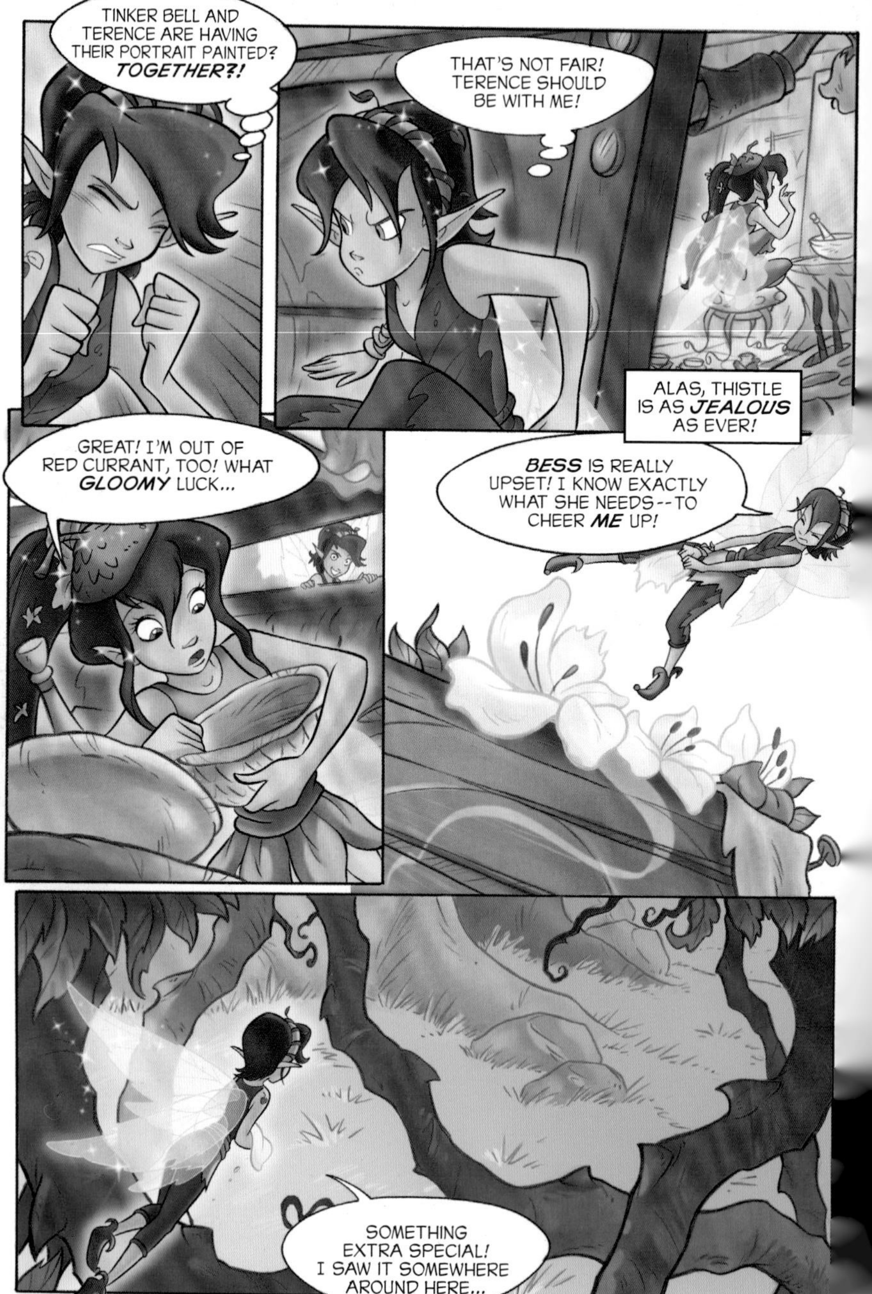
TINKER BELL AND TERENCE ARE HAVING THEIR PORTRAIT PAINTED? *TOGETHER?!*
THAT'S NOT FAIR! TERENCE SHOULD BE WITH ME!
ALAS, THISTLE IS AS *JEALOUS* AS EVER!
GREAT! I'M OUT OF RED CURRANT, TOO! WHAT *GLOOMY* LUCK...
BESS IS REALLY UPSET! I KNOW EXACTLY WHAT SHE NEEDS--TO CHEER *ME* UP!
SOMETHING EXTRA SPECIAL! I SAW IT SOMEWHERE AROUND HERE...

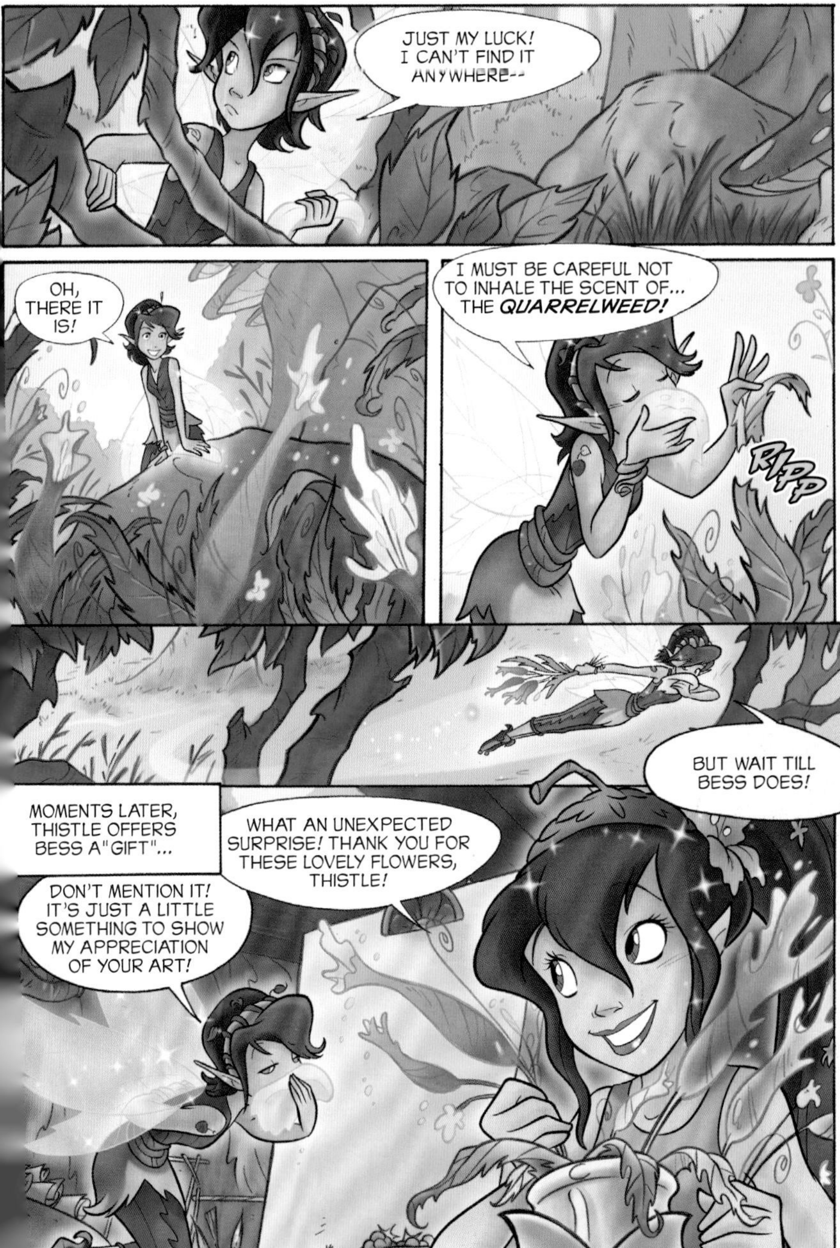
JUST MY LUCK! I CAN'T FIND IT ANYWHERE--
OH, THERE IT IS!
I MUST BE CAREFUL NOT TO INHALE THE SCENT OF... THE QUARRELWEED!
RIPP
BUT WAIT TILL BESS DOES!
MOMENTS LATER, THISTLE OFFERS BESS A"GIFT"...
WHAT AN UNEXPECTED SURPRISE! THANK YOU FOR THESE LOVELY FLOWERS, THISTLE!
DON'T MENTION IT! IT'S JUST A LITTLE SOMETHING TO SHOW MY APPRECIATION OF YOUR ART!

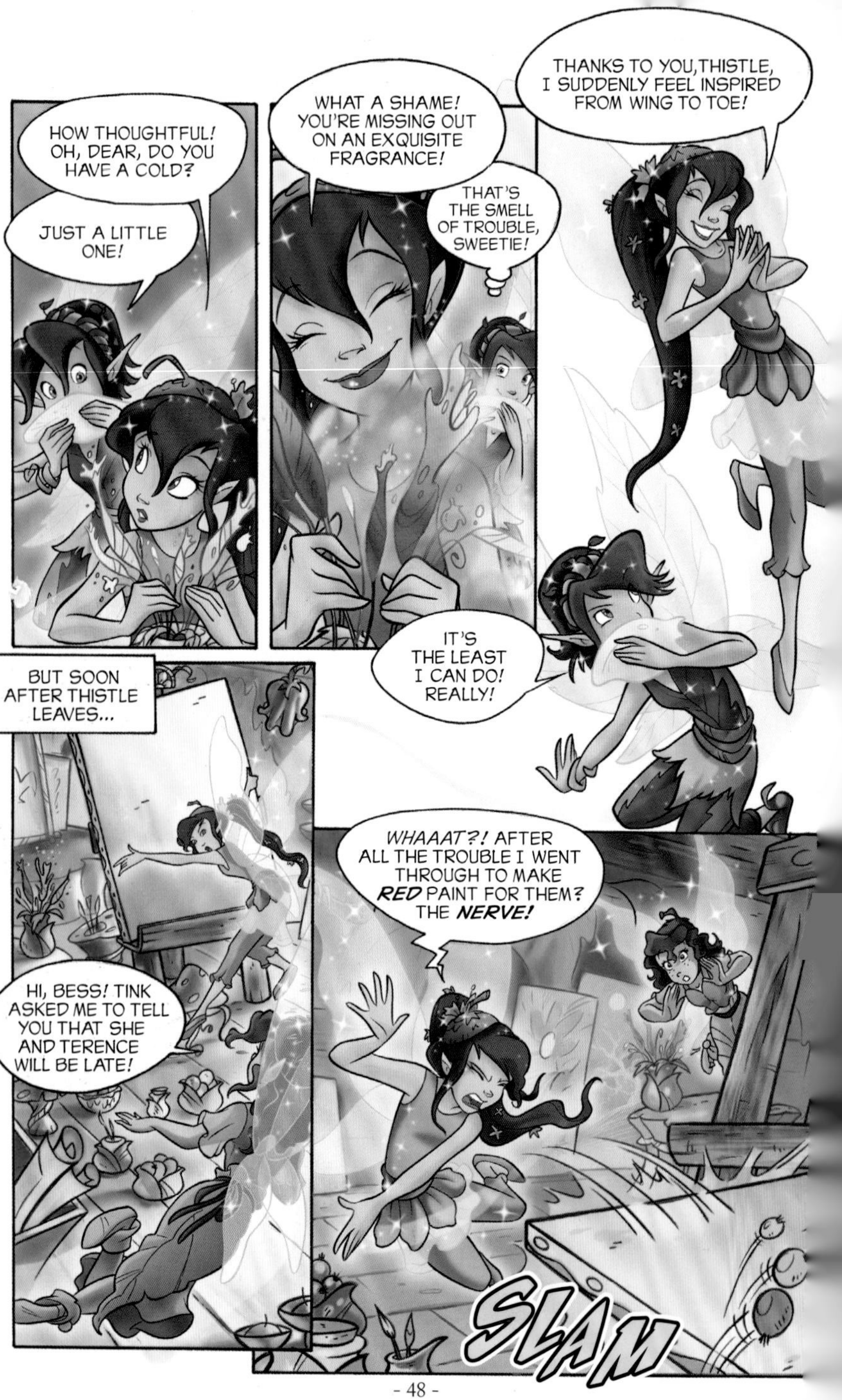
HOW THOUGHTFUL! OH, DEAR, DO YOU HAVE A COLD?
JUST A LITTLE ONE!
WHAT A SHAME! YOU'RE MISSING OUT ON AN EXQUISITE FRAGRANCE!
THAT'S THE SMELL OF TROUBLE, SWEETIE!
THANKS TO YOU, THISTLE, I SUDDENLY FEEL INSPIRED FROM WING TO TOE!
IT'S THE LEAST I CAN DO! REALLY!
BUT SOON AFTER THISTLE LEAVES...
HI, BESS! TINK ASKED ME TO TELL YOU THAT SHE AND TERENCE WILL BE LATE!
WHAAAT?! AFTER ALL THE TROUBLE I WENT THROUGH TO MAKE ***RED*** PAINT FOR THEM? THE ***NERVE!***
SLAM

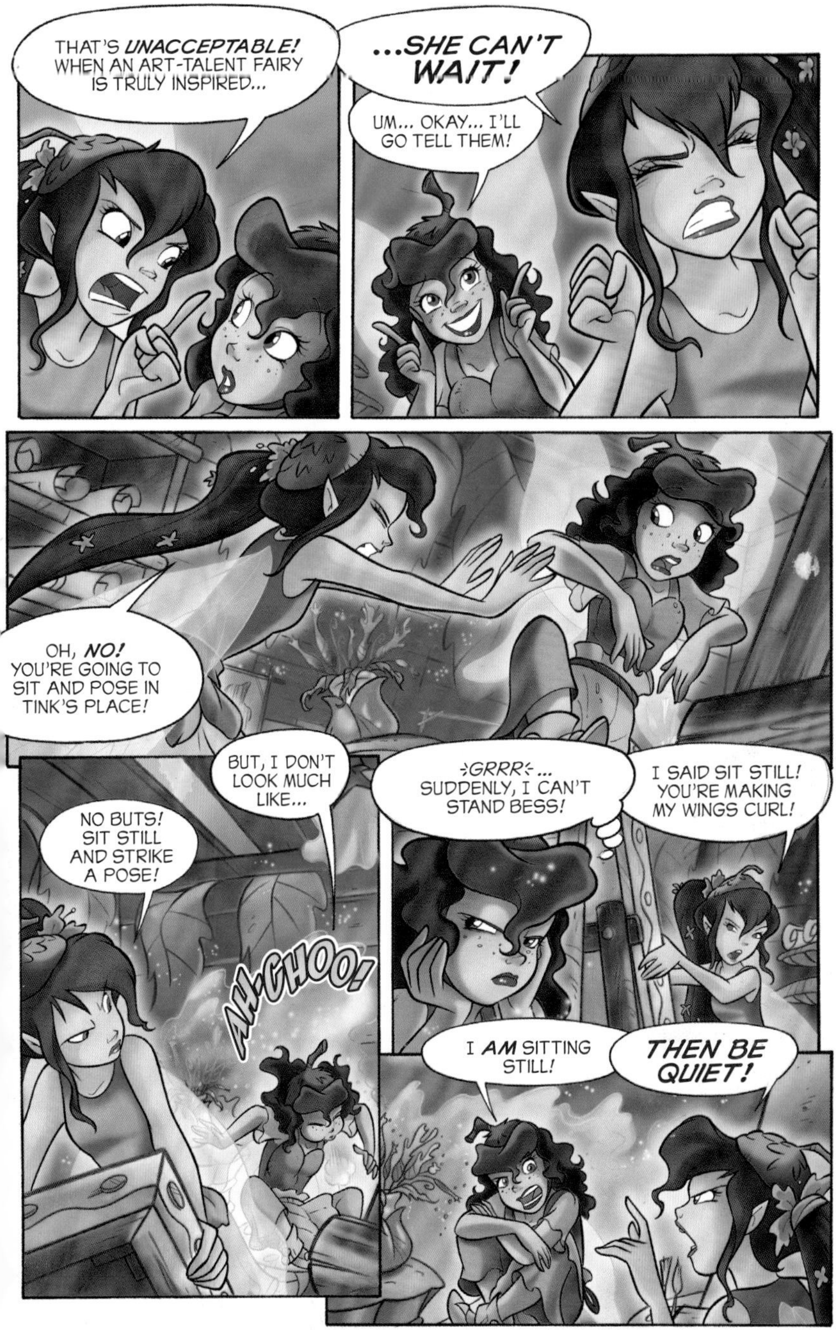
THAT'S UNACCEPTABLE! WHEN AN ART-TALENT FAIRY IS TRULY INSPIRED...
...SHE CAN'T WAIT!
UM... OKAY... I'LL GO TELL THEM!
OH, NO! YOU'RE GOING TO SIT AND POSE IN TINK'S PLACE!
BUT, I DON'T LOOK MUCH LIKE...
NO BUTS! SIT STILL AND STRIKE A POSE!
AH-CHOO!
GRRR... SUDDENLY, I CAN'T STAND BESS!
I SAID SIT STILL! YOU'RE MAKING MY WINGS CURL!
I AM SITTING STILL!
THEN BE QUIET!

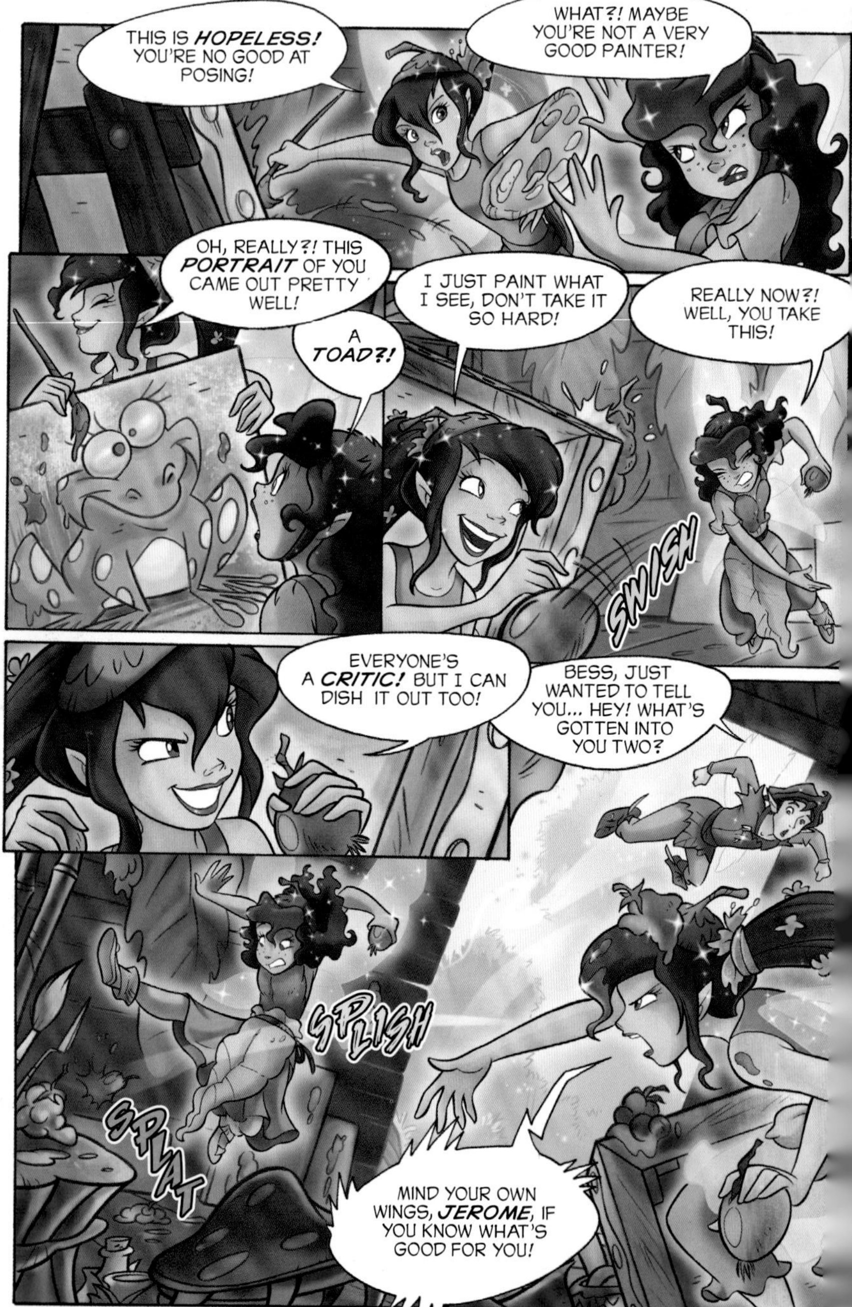
THIS IS HOPELESS! YOU'RE NO GOOD AT POSING!
WHAT?! MAYBE YOU'RE NOT A VERY GOOD PAINTER!
OH, REALLY?! THIS PORTRAIT OF YOU CAME OUT PRETTY WELL!
A TOAD?!
I JUST PAINT WHAT I SEE, DON'T TAKE IT SO HARD!
REALLY NOW?! WELL, YOU TAKE THIS!
SWISH
EVERYONE'S A CRITIC! BUT I CAN DISH IT OUT TOO!
BESS, JUST WANTED TO TELL YOU... HEY! WHAT'S GOTTEN INTO YOU TWO?
SPLISH
SPLAT
MIND YOUR OWN WINGS, JEROME, IF YOU KNOW WHAT'S GOOD FOR YOU!

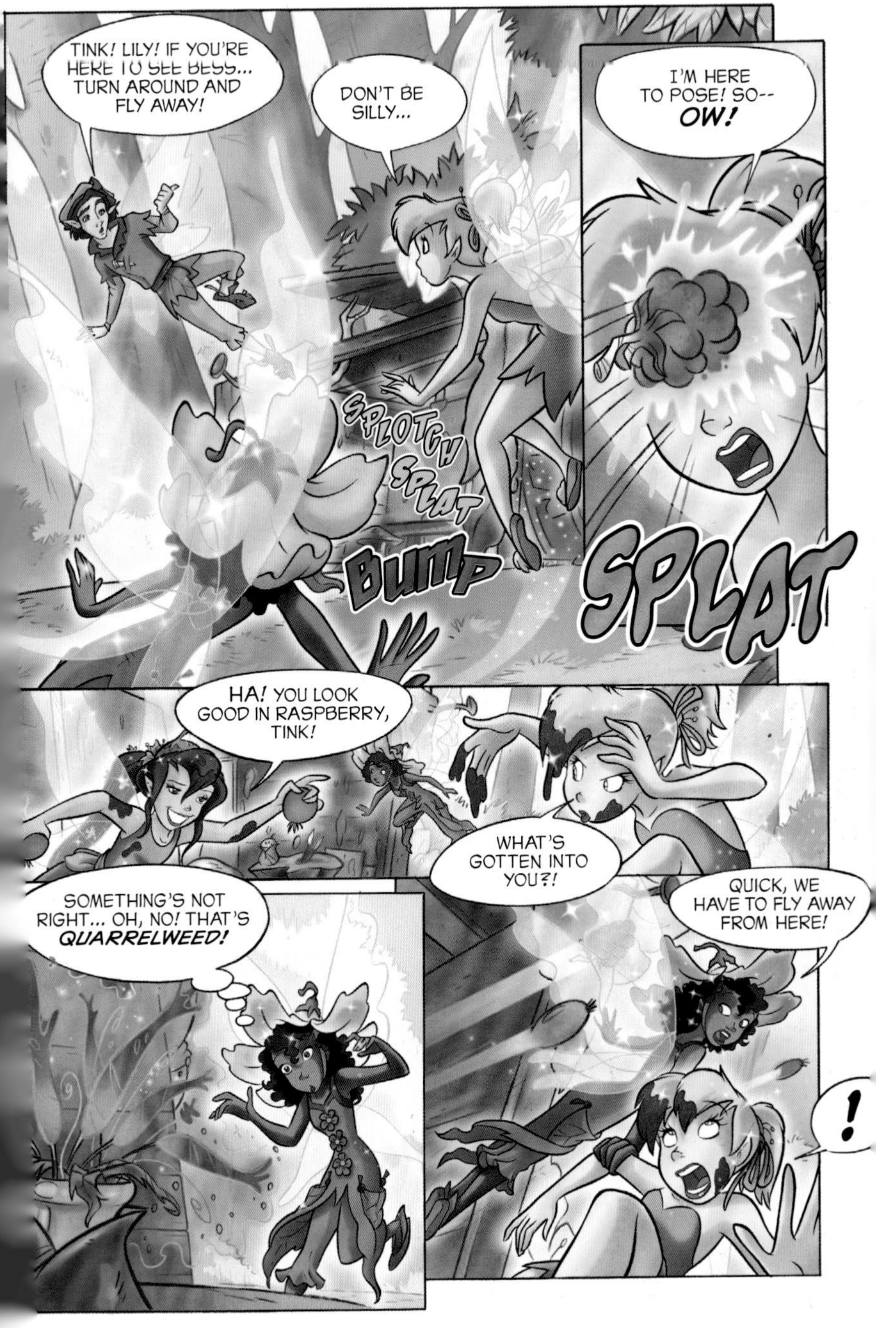

TINK! LILY! IF YOU'RE HERE TO SEE BESS... TURN AROUND AND FLY AWAY!
DON'T BE SILLY...
I'M HERE TO POSE! SO-- OW!
SPLOTCH
SPLAT
BUMP
SPLAT
HA! YOU LOOK GOOD IN RASPBERRY, TINK!
WHAT'S GOTTEN INTO YOU?!
SOMETHING'S NOT RIGHT... OH, NO! THAT'S QUARRELWEED!
QUICK, WE HAVE TO FLY AWAY FROM HERE!
!

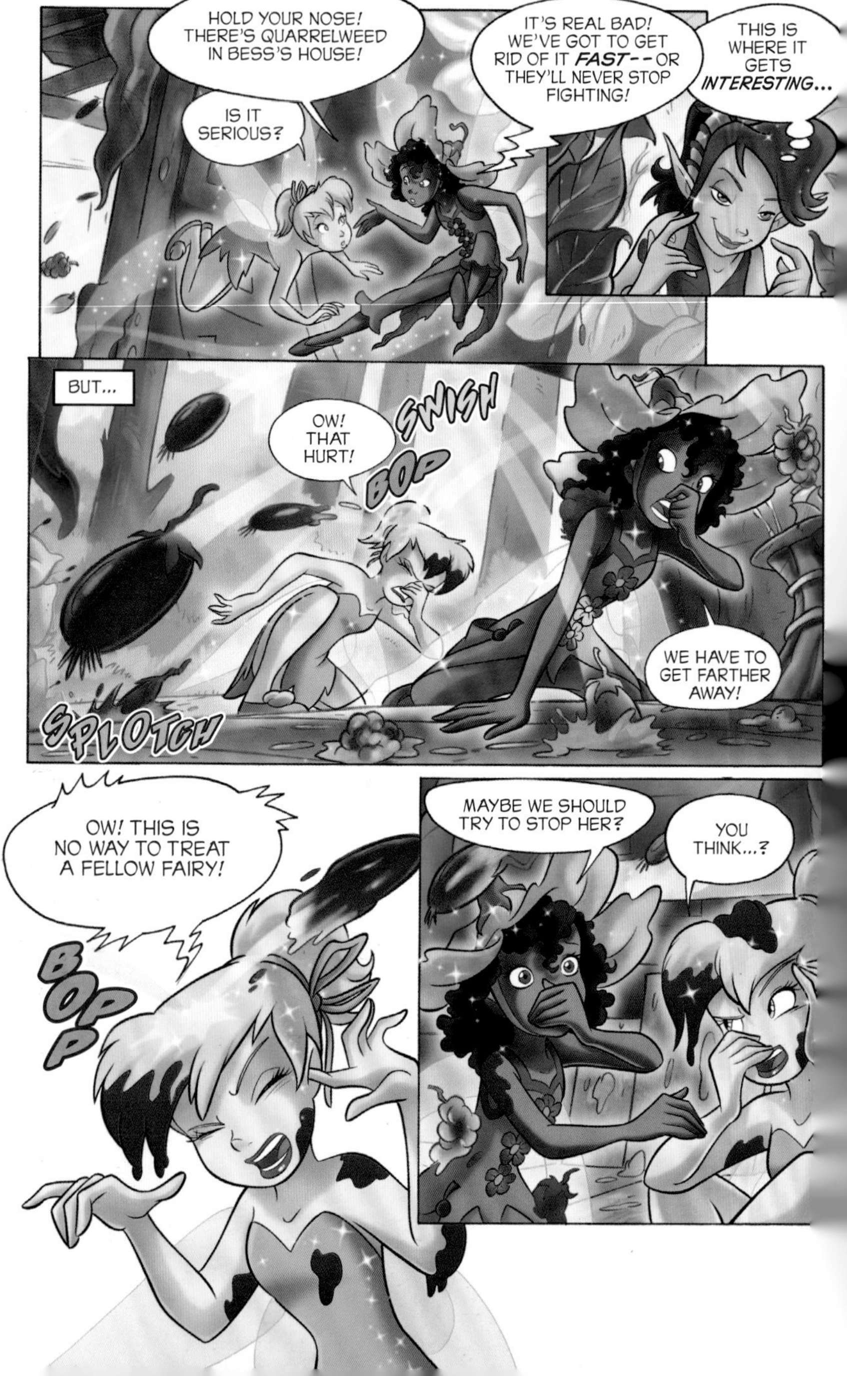
HOLD YOUR NOSE! THERE'S QUARRELWEED IN BESS'S HOUSE!
IS IT SERIOUS?
IT'S REAL BAD! WE'VE GOT TO GET RID OF IT FAST--OR THEY'LL NEVER STOP FIGHTING!
THIS IS WHERE IT GETS INTERESTING...
BUT...
OW! THAT HURT!
SWISH
BOP
SPLOTCH
WE HAVE TO GET FARTHER AWAY!
OW! THIS IS NO WAY TO TREAT A FELLOW FAIRY!
BOP
MAYBE WE SHOULD TRY TO STOP HER?
YOU THINK...?

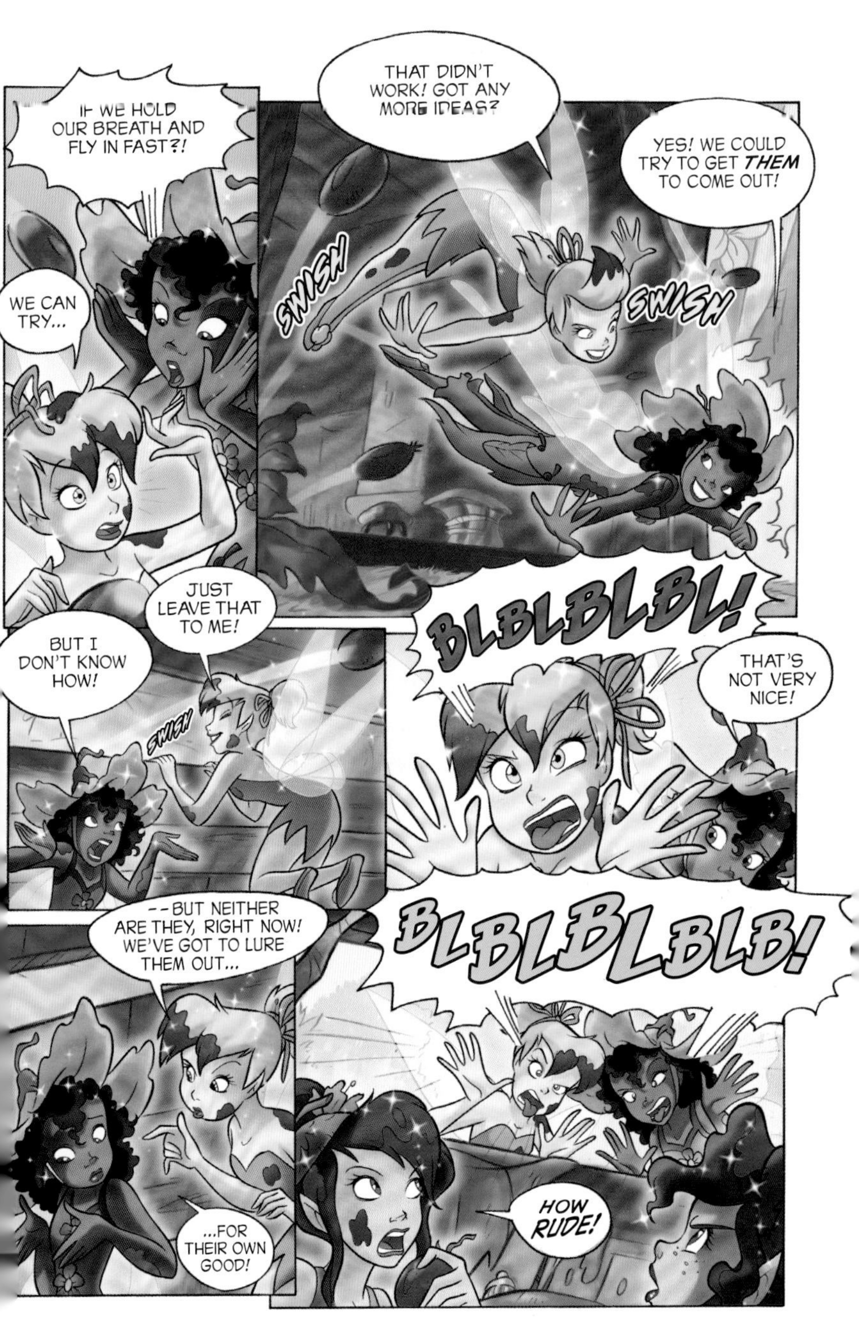
IF WE HOLD OUR BREATH AND FLY IN FAST?!
WE CAN TRY...
THAT DIDN'T WORK! GOT ANY MORE IDEAS?
YES! WE COULD TRY TO GET *THEM* TO COME OUT!
SWISH
SWISH
BUT I DON'T KNOW HOW!
JUST LEAVE THAT TO ME!
SWISH
BLBLBLBL!
THAT'S NOT VERY NICE!
--BUT NEITHER ARE THEY, RIGHT NOW! WE'VE GOT TO LURE THEM OUT...
...FOR THEIR OWN GOOD!
BLBLBLBLB!
HOW RUDE!

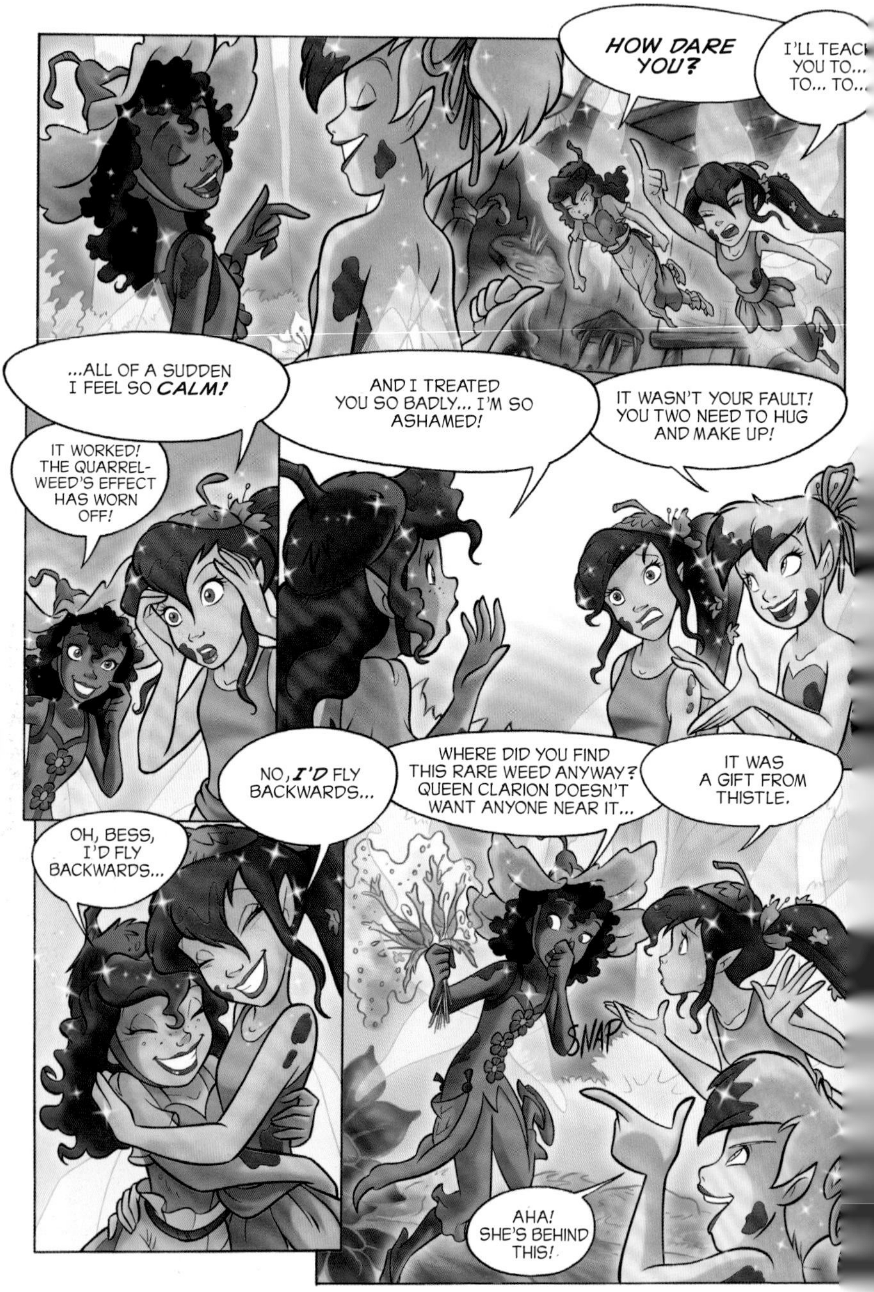
HOW DARE YOU?
I'LL TEACH YOU TO... TO... TO...
...ALL OF A SUDDEN I FEEL SO CALM!
AND I TREATED YOU SO BADLY... I'M SO ASHAMED!
IT WORKED! THE QUARREL-WEED'S EFFECT HAS WORN OFF!
IT WASN'T YOUR FAULT! YOU TWO NEED TO HUG AND MAKE UP!
OH, BESS, I'D FLY BACKWARDS...
NO, I'D FLY BACKWARDS...
WHERE DID YOU FIND THIS RARE WEED ANYWAY? QUEEN CLARION DOESN'T WANT ANYONE NEAR IT...
IT WAS A GIFT FROM THISTLE.
SNAP
AHA! SHE'S BEHIND THIS!

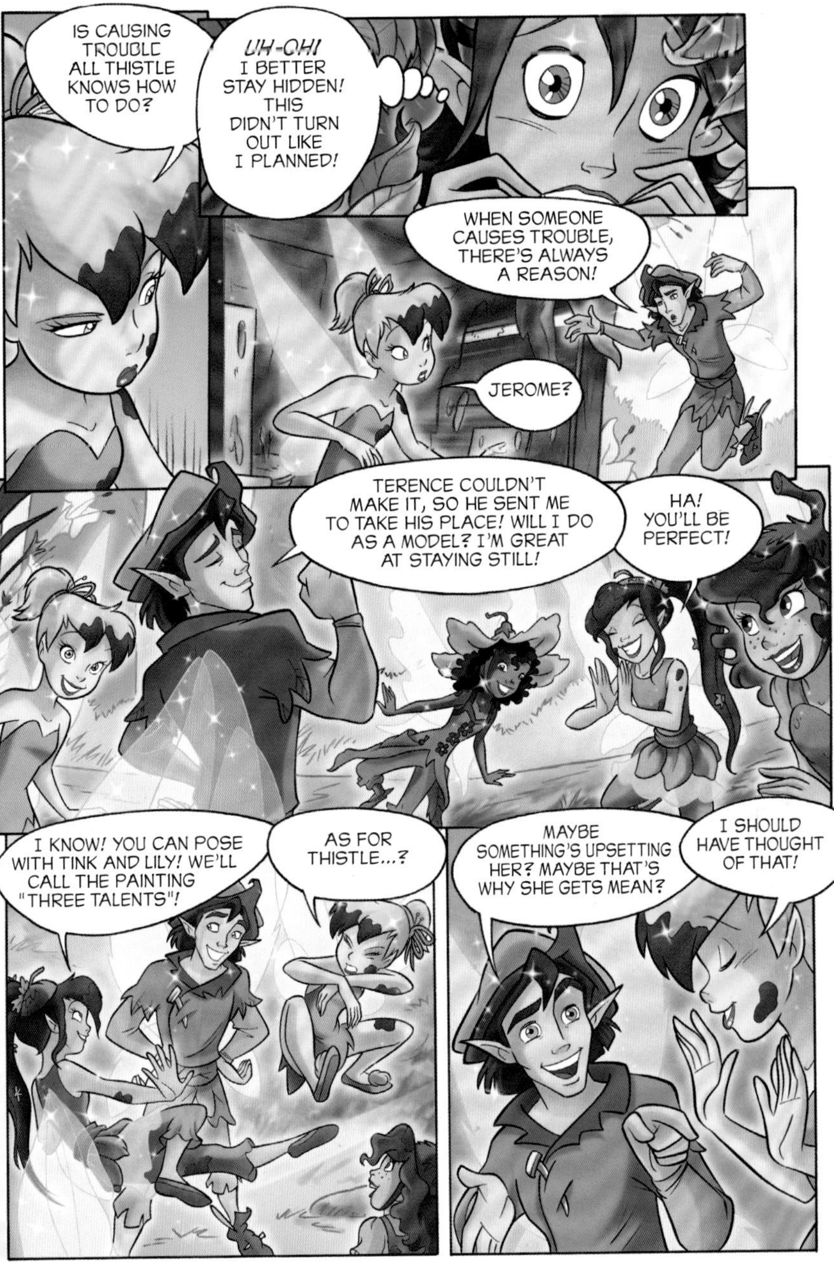
IS CAUSING TROUBLE ALL THISTLE KNOWS HOW TO DO?
UH-OH! I BETTER STAY HIDDEN! THIS DIDN'T TURN OUT LIKE I PLANNED!
WHEN SOMEONE CAUSES TROUBLE, THERE'S ALWAYS A REASON!
JEROME?
TERENCE COULDN'T MAKE IT, SO HE SENT ME TO TAKE HIS PLACE! WILL I DO AS A MODEL? I'M GREAT AT STAYING STILL!
HA! YOU'LL BE PERFECT!
I KNOW! YOU CAN POSE WITH TINK AND LILY! WE'LL CALL THE PAINTING "THREE TALENTS"!
AS FOR THISTLE...?
MAYBE SOMETHING'S UPSETTING HER? MAYBE THAT'S WHY SHE GETS MEAN?
I SHOULD HAVE THOUGHT OF THAT!

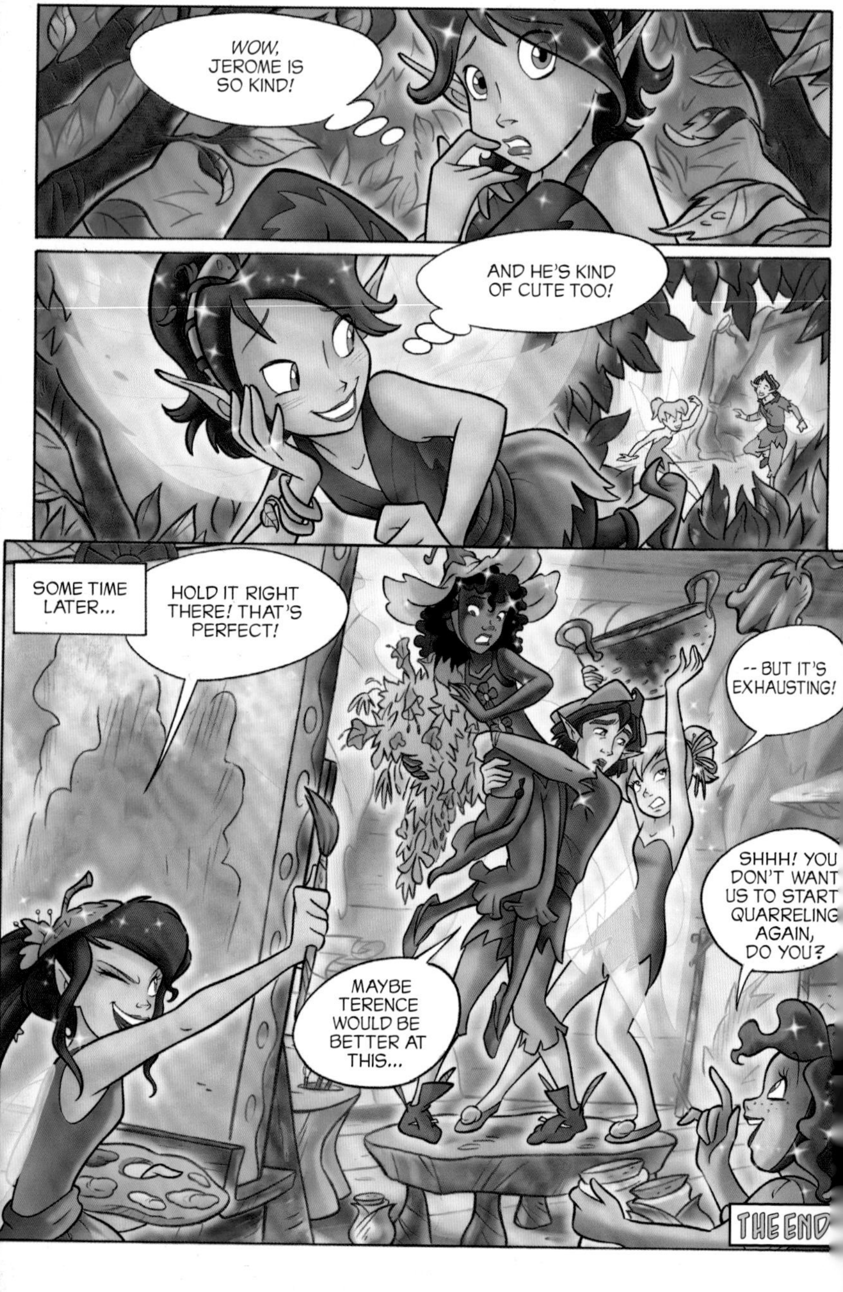
WOW, JEROME IS SO KIND!
AND HE'S KIND OF CUTE TOO!
SOME TIME LATER...
HOLD IT RIGHT THERE! THAT'S PERFECT!
-- BUT IT'S EXHAUSTING!
MAYBE TERENCE WOULD BE BETTER AT THIS...
SHHH! YOU DON'T WANT US TO START QUARRELING AGAIN, DO YOU?
THE END

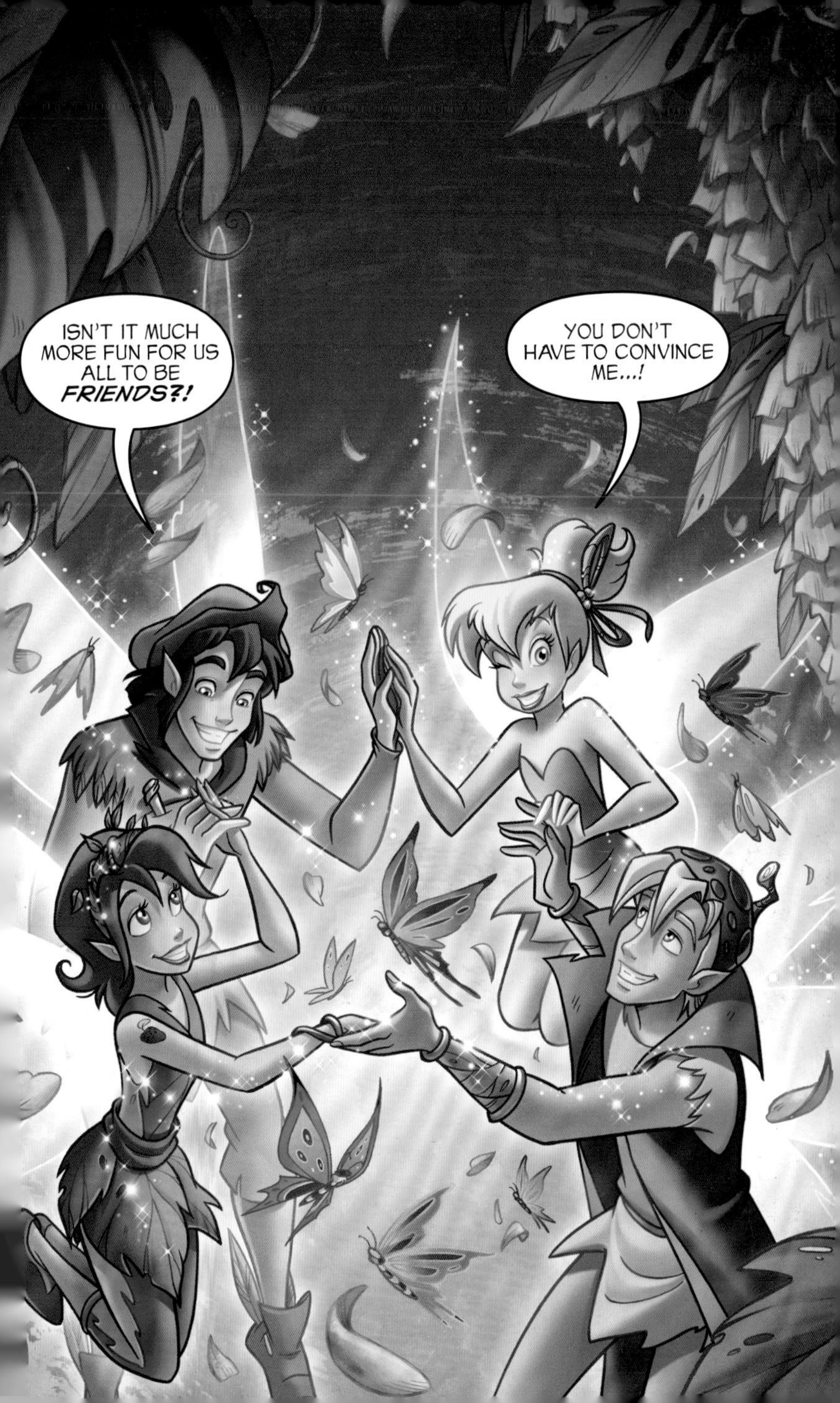
ISN'T IT MUCH MORE FUN FOR US ALL TO BE *FRIENDS?!*
YOU DON'T HAVE TO CONVINCE ME...!

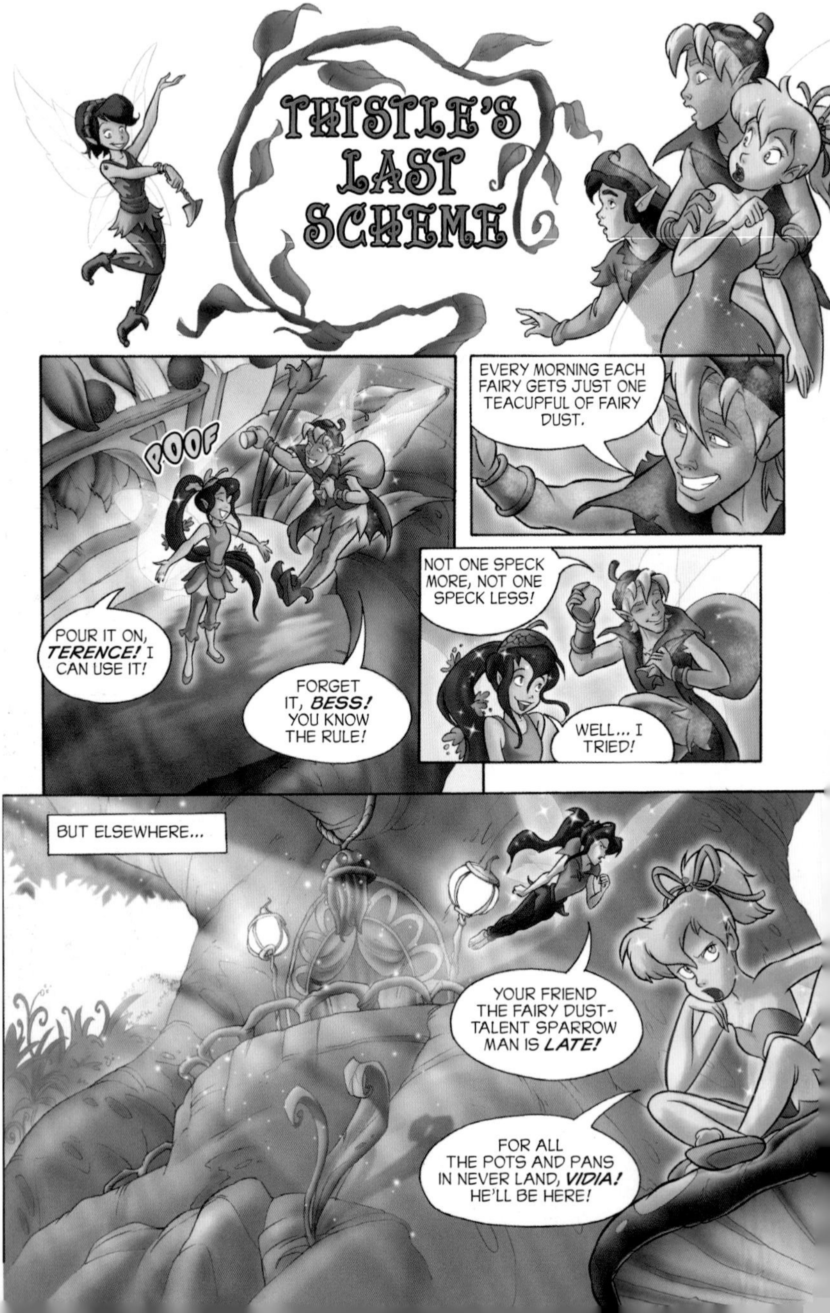
THISTLE'S LAST SCHEME
POOF
POUR IT ON, TERENCE! I CAN USE IT!
FORGET IT, BESS! YOU KNOW THE RULE!
EVERY MORNING EACH FAIRY GETS JUST ONE TEACUPFUL OF FAIRY DUST.
NOT ONE SPECK MORE, NOT ONE SPECK LESS!
WELL... I TRIED!
BUT ELSEWHERE...
YOUR FRIEND THE FAIRY DUST-TALENT SPARROW MAN IS LATE!
FOR ALL THE POTS AND PANS IN NEVER LAND, VIDIA! HE'LL BE HERE!

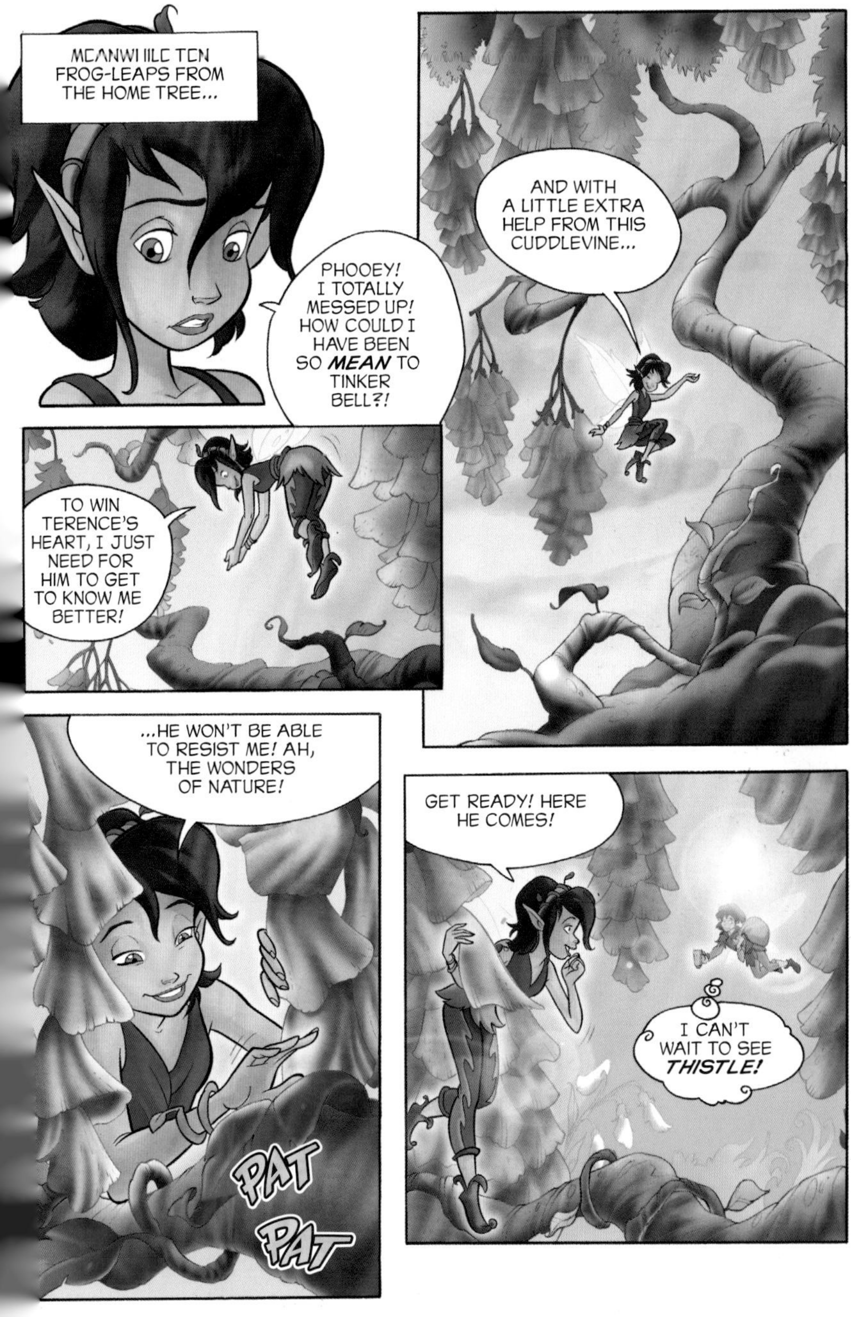
MEANWHILE TEN FROG-LEAPS FROM THE HOME TREE...
PHOOEY! I TOTALLY MESSED UP! HOW COULD I HAVE BEEN SO *MEAN* TO TINKER BELL?!
TO WIN TERENCE'S HEART, I JUST NEED FOR HIM TO GET TO KNOW ME BETTER!
AND WITH A LITTLE EXTRA HELP FROM THIS CUDDLEVINE...
...HE WON'T BE ABLE TO RESIST ME! AH, THE WONDERS OF NATURE!
PAT
PAT
GET READY! HERE HE COMES!
I CAN'T WAIT TO SEE *THISTLE!*

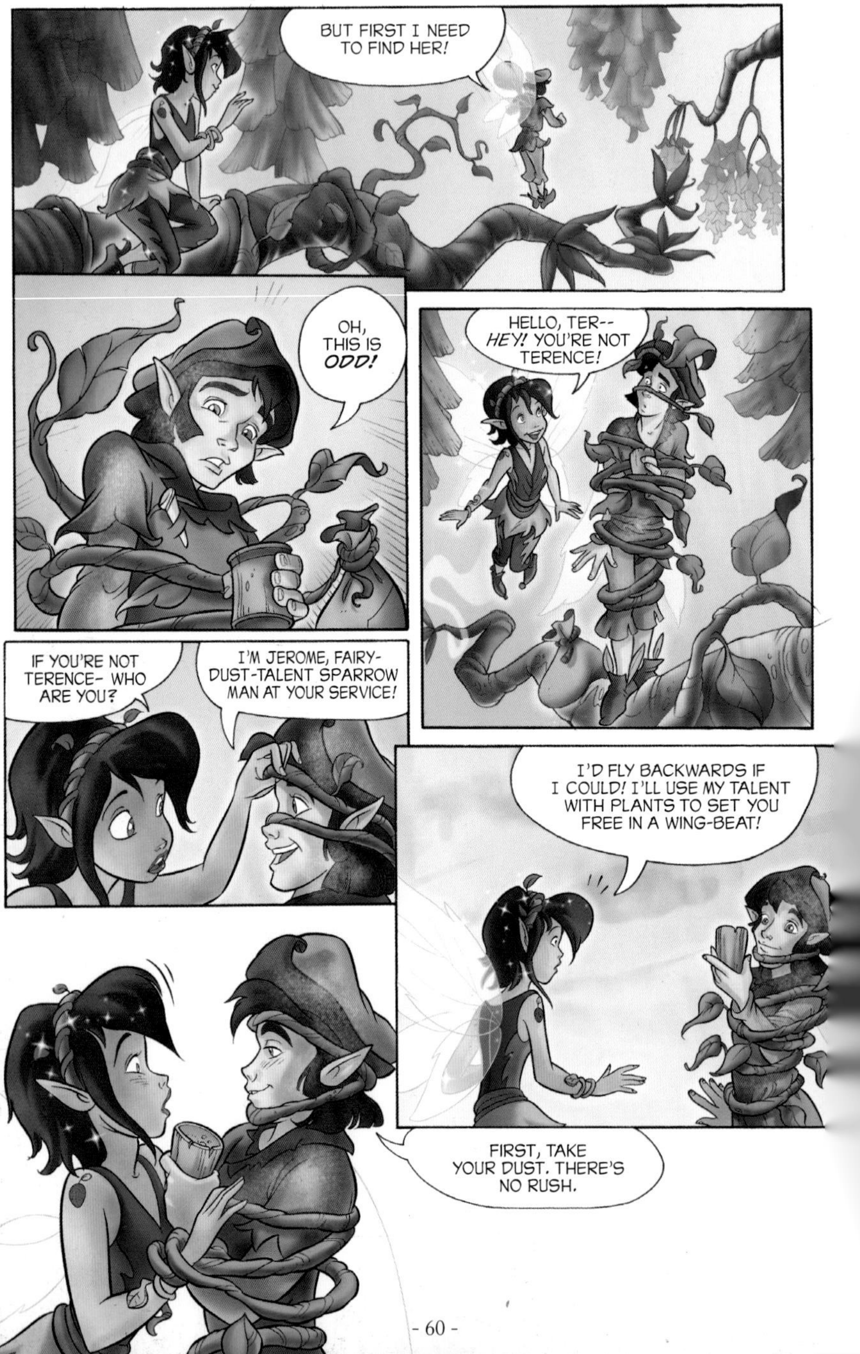
BUT FIRST I NEED TO FIND HER!
OH, THIS IS ODD!
HELLO, TER-- HEY! YOU'RE NOT TERENCE!
IF YOU'RE NOT TERENCE- WHO ARE YOU?
I'M JEROME, FAIRY-DUST-TALENT SPARROW MAN AT YOUR SERVICE!
I'D FLY BACKWARDS IF I COULD! I'LL USE MY TALENT WITH PLANTS TO SET YOU FREE IN A WING-BEAT!
FIRST, TAKE YOUR DUST. THERE'S NO RUSH.

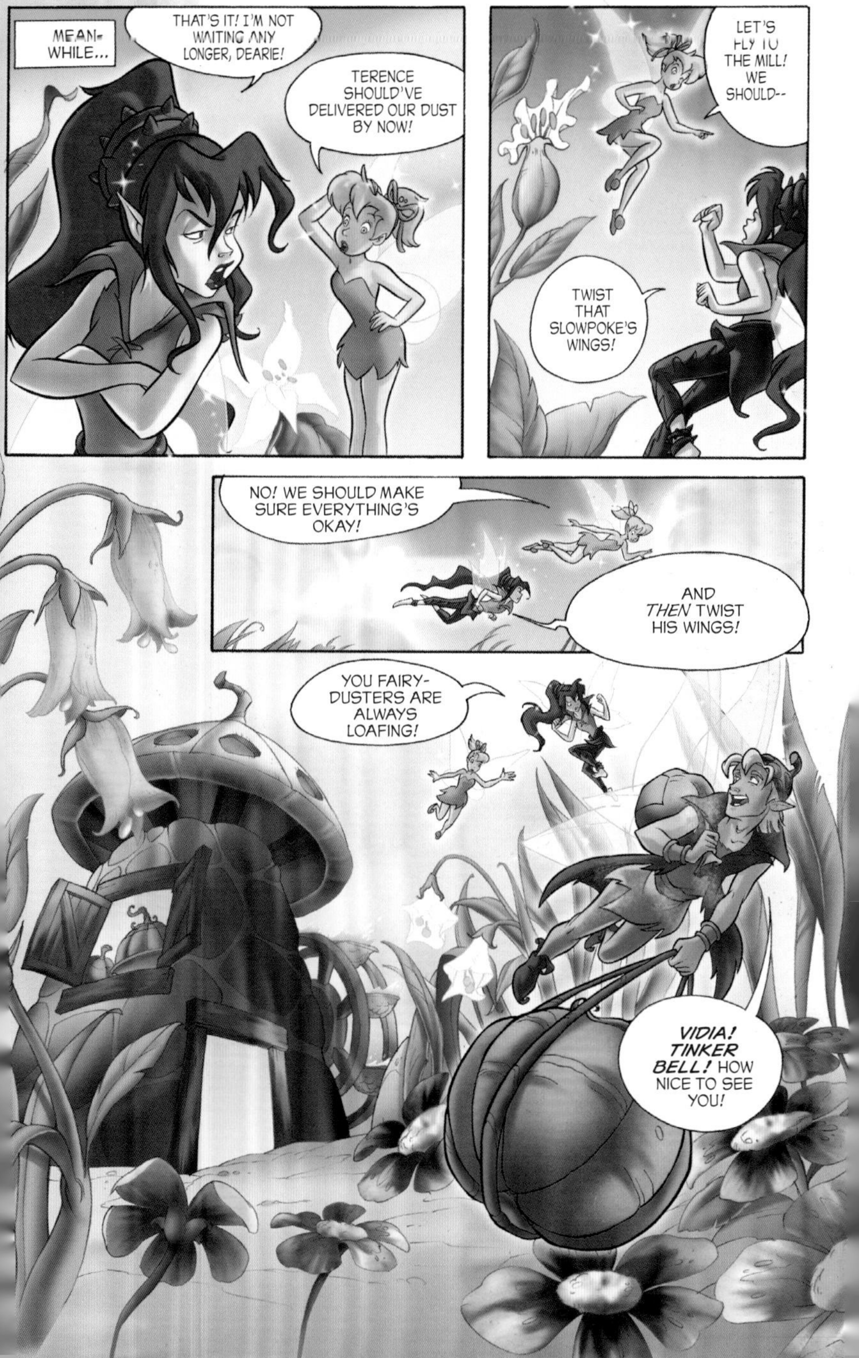
MEAN-WHILE...
THAT'S IT! I'M NOT WAITING ANY LONGER, DEARIE!
TERENCE SHOULD'VE DELIVERED OUR DUST BY NOW!
LET'S FLY TO THE MILL! WE SHOULD--
TWIST THAT SLOWPOKE'S WINGS!
NO! WE SHOULD MAKE SURE EVERYTHING'S OKAY!
AND *THEN* TWIST HIS WINGS!
YOU FAIRY-DUSTERS ARE ALWAYS LOAFING!
VIDIA! TINKER BELL! HOW NICE TO SEE YOU!

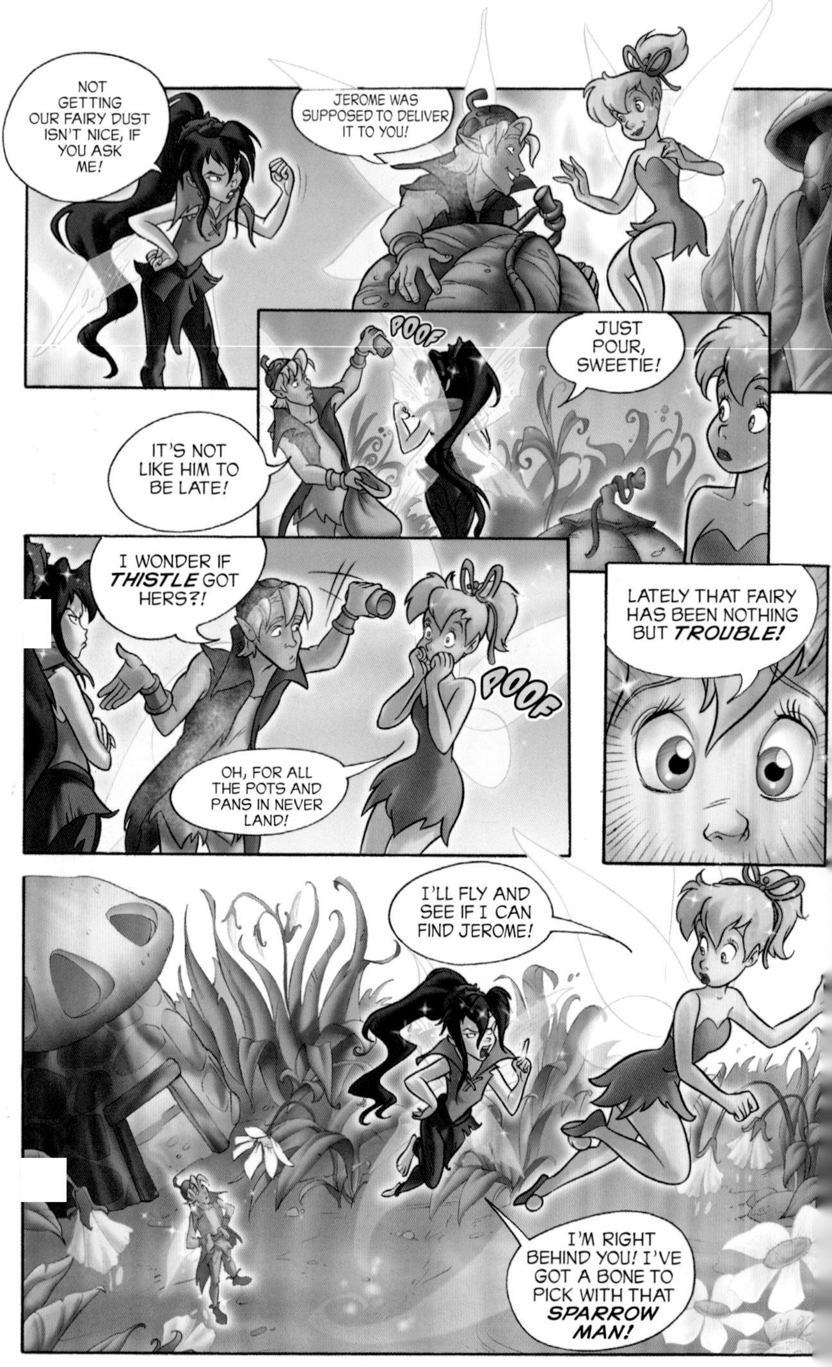
NOT GETTING OUR FAIRY DUST ISN'T NICE, IF YOU ASK ME!
JEROME WAS SUPPOSED TO DELIVER IT TO YOU!
POOF
JUST POUR, SWEETIE!
IT'S NOT LIKE HIM TO BE LATE!
I WONDER IF THISTLE GOT HERS?!
POOF
OH, FOR ALL THE POTS AND PANS IN NEVER LAND!
LATELY THAT FAIRY HAS BEEN NOTHING BUT TROUBLE!
I'LL FLY AND SEE IF I CAN FIND JEROME!
I'M RIGHT BEHIND YOU! I'VE GOT A BONE TO PICK WITH THAT SPARROW MAN!

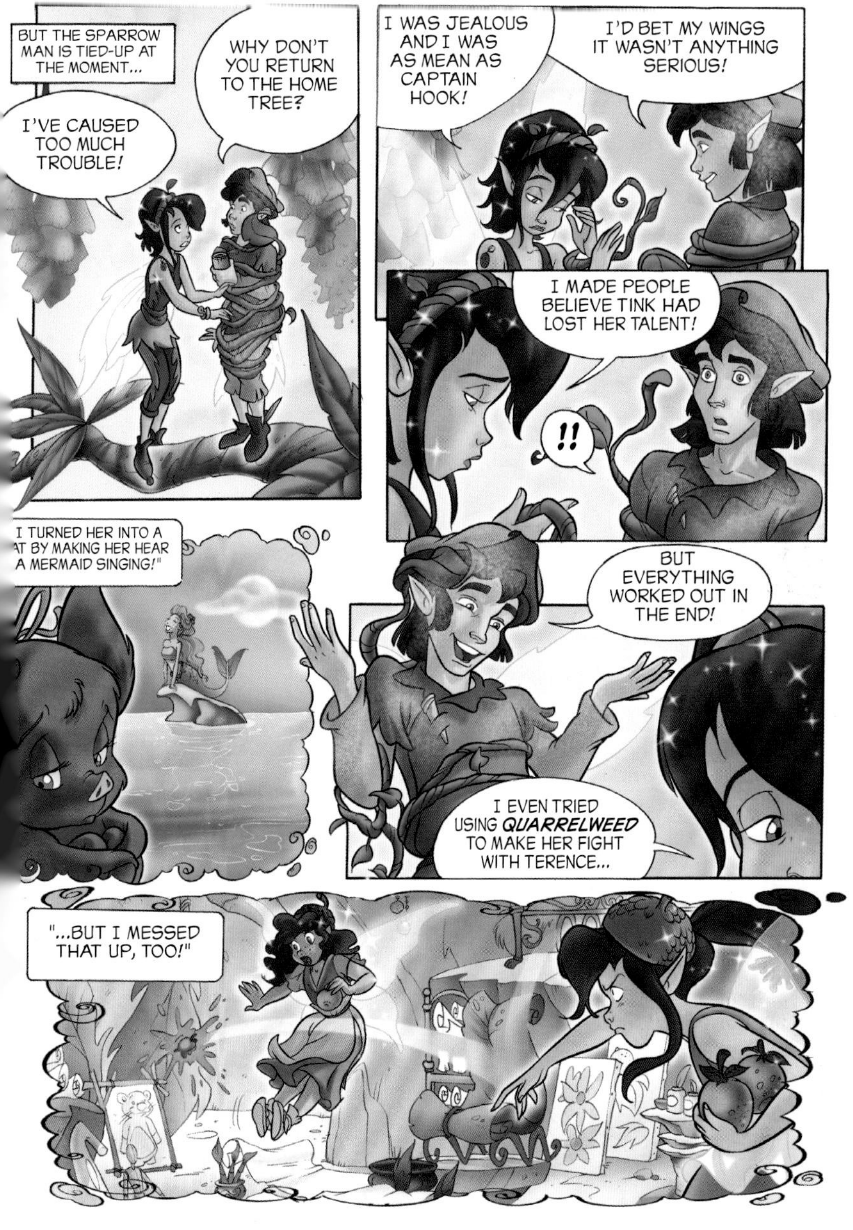
BUT THE SPARROW MAN IS TIED-UP AT THE MOMENT...
WHY DON'T YOU RETURN TO THE HOME TREE?
I'VE CAUSED TOO MUCH TROUBLE!
I WAS JEALOUS AND I WAS AS MEAN AS CAPTAIN HOOK!
I'D BET MY WINGS IT WASN'T ANYTHING SERIOUS!
I MADE PEOPLE BELIEVE TINK HAD LOST HER TALENT!
!!
I TURNED HER INTO A
AT BY MAKING HER HEAR
A MERMAID SINGING!"
BUT EVERYTHING WORKED OUT IN THE END!
I EVEN TRIED USING ***QUARRELWEED*** TO MAKE HER FIGHT WITH TERENCE...
"...BUT I MESSED THAT UP, TOO!"

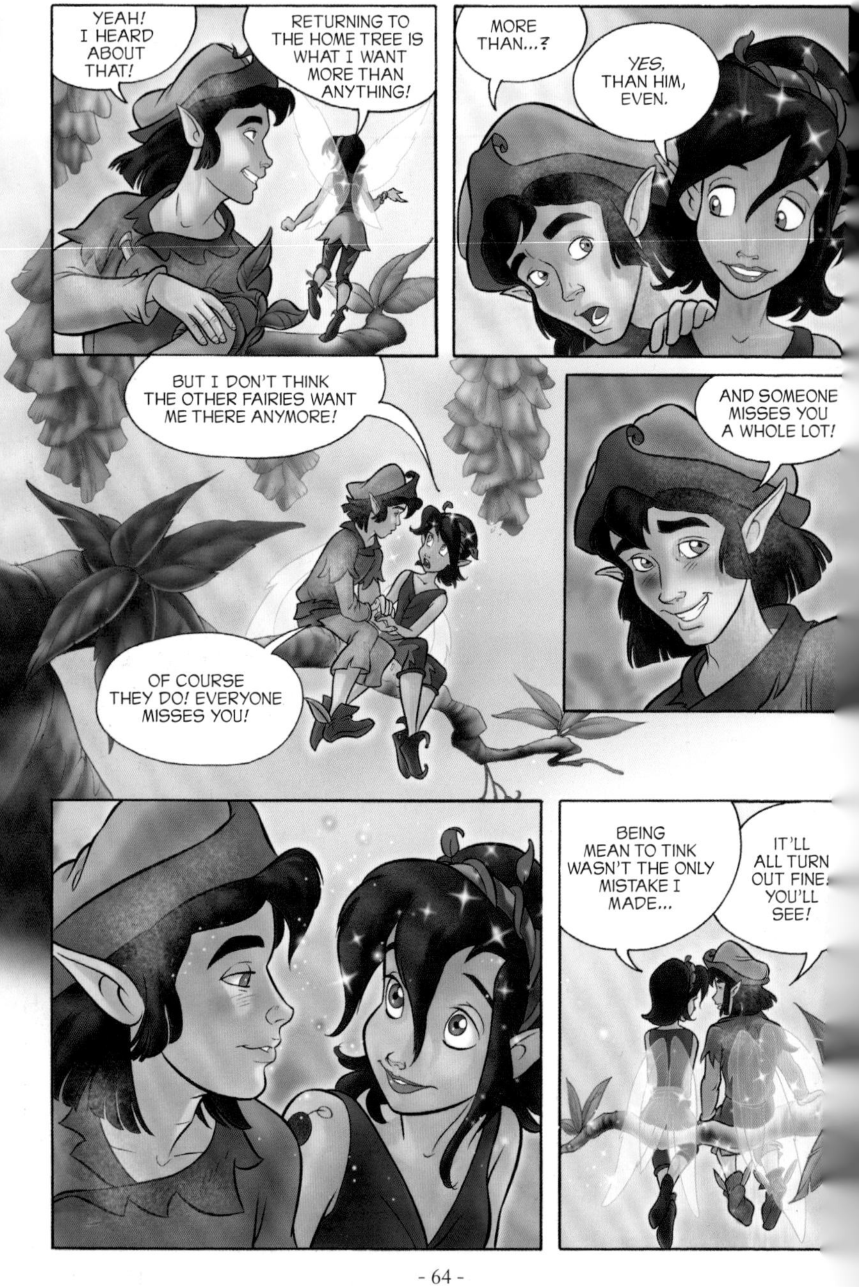
YEAH! I HEARD ABOUT THAT!
RETURNING TO THE HOME TREE IS WHAT I WANT MORE THAN ANYTHING!
MORE THAN...?
YES, THAN HIM, EVEN.
BUT I DON'T THINK THE OTHER FAIRIES WANT ME THERE ANYMORE!
OF COURSE THEY DO! EVERYONE MISSES YOU!
AND SOMEONE MISSES YOU A WHOLE LOT!
BEING MEAN TO TINK WASN'T THE ONLY MISTAKE I MADE...
IT'LL ALL TURN OUT FINE! YOU'LL SEE!

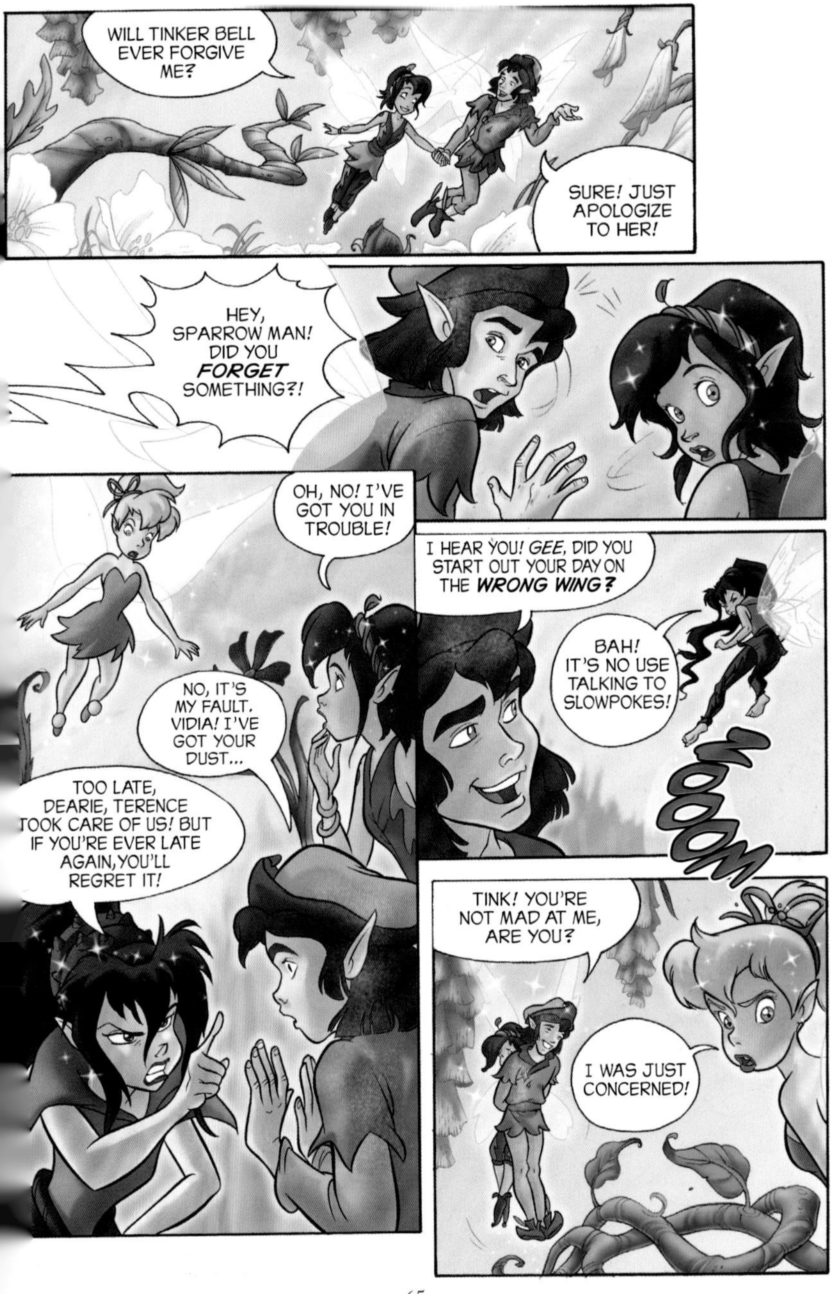
WILL TINKER BELL EVER FORGIVE ME?
SURE! JUST APOLOGIZE TO HER!
HEY, SPARROW MAN! DID YOU FORGET SOMETHING?!
OH, NO! I'VE GOT YOU IN TROUBLE!
NO, IT'S MY FAULT. VIDIA! I'VE GOT YOUR DUST...
TOO LATE, DEARIE, TERENCE TOOK CARE OF US! BUT IF YOU'RE EVER LATE AGAIN, YOU'LL REGRET IT!
I HEAR YOU! GEE, DID YOU START OUT YOUR DAY ON THE WRONG WING?
BAH! IT'S NO USE TALKING TO SLOWPOKES!
VOOOM
TINK! YOU'RE NOT MAD AT ME, ARE YOU?
I WAS JUST CONCERNED!

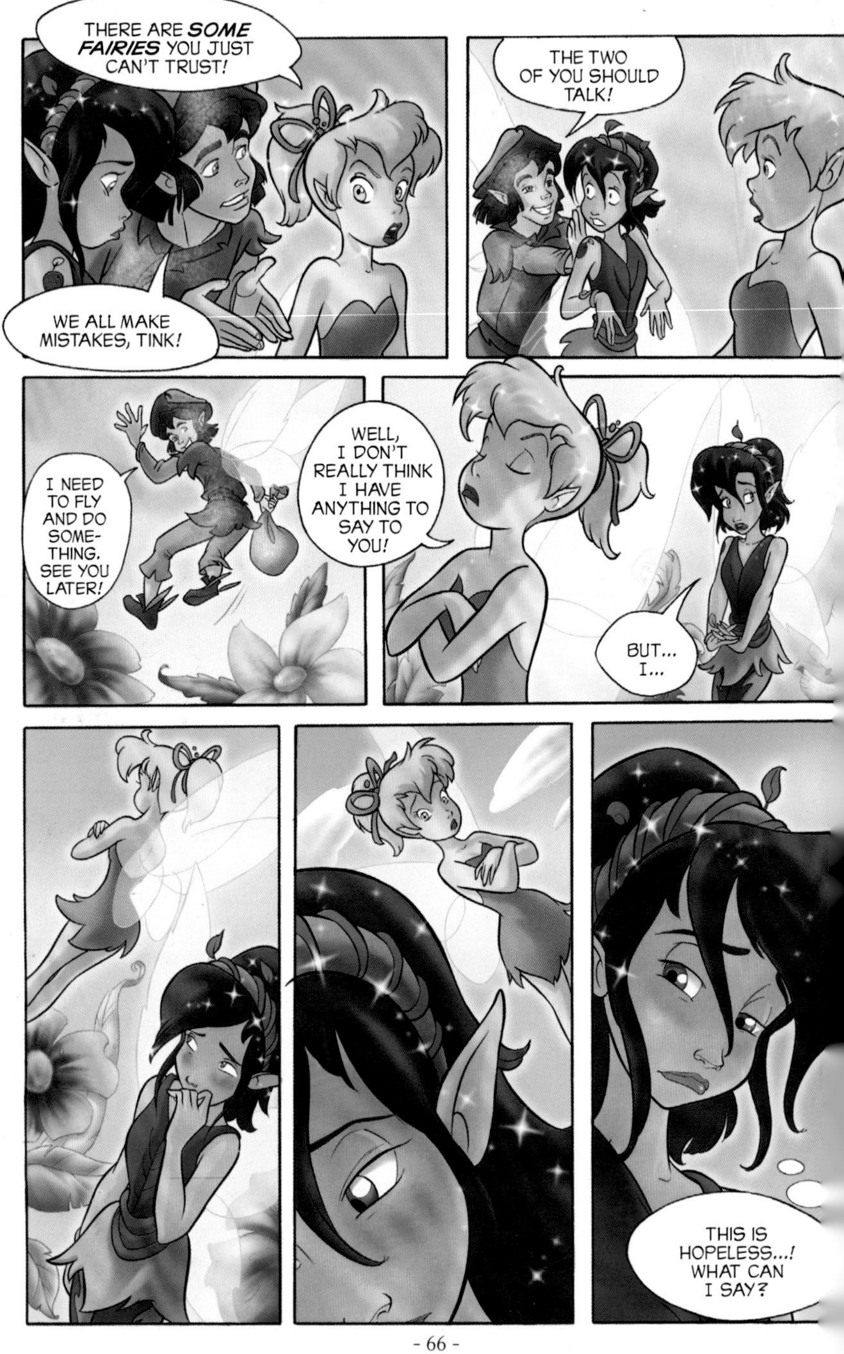

THERE ARE **SOME FAIRIES** YOU JUST CAN'T TRUST!
WE ALL MAKE MISTAKES, TINK!
THE TWO OF YOU SHOULD TALK!
I NEED TO FLY AND DO SOME-THING. SEE YOU LATER!
WELL, I DON'T REALLY THINK I HAVE ANYTHING TO SAY TO YOU!
BUT... I...
THIS IS HOPELESS...! WHAT CAN I SAY?

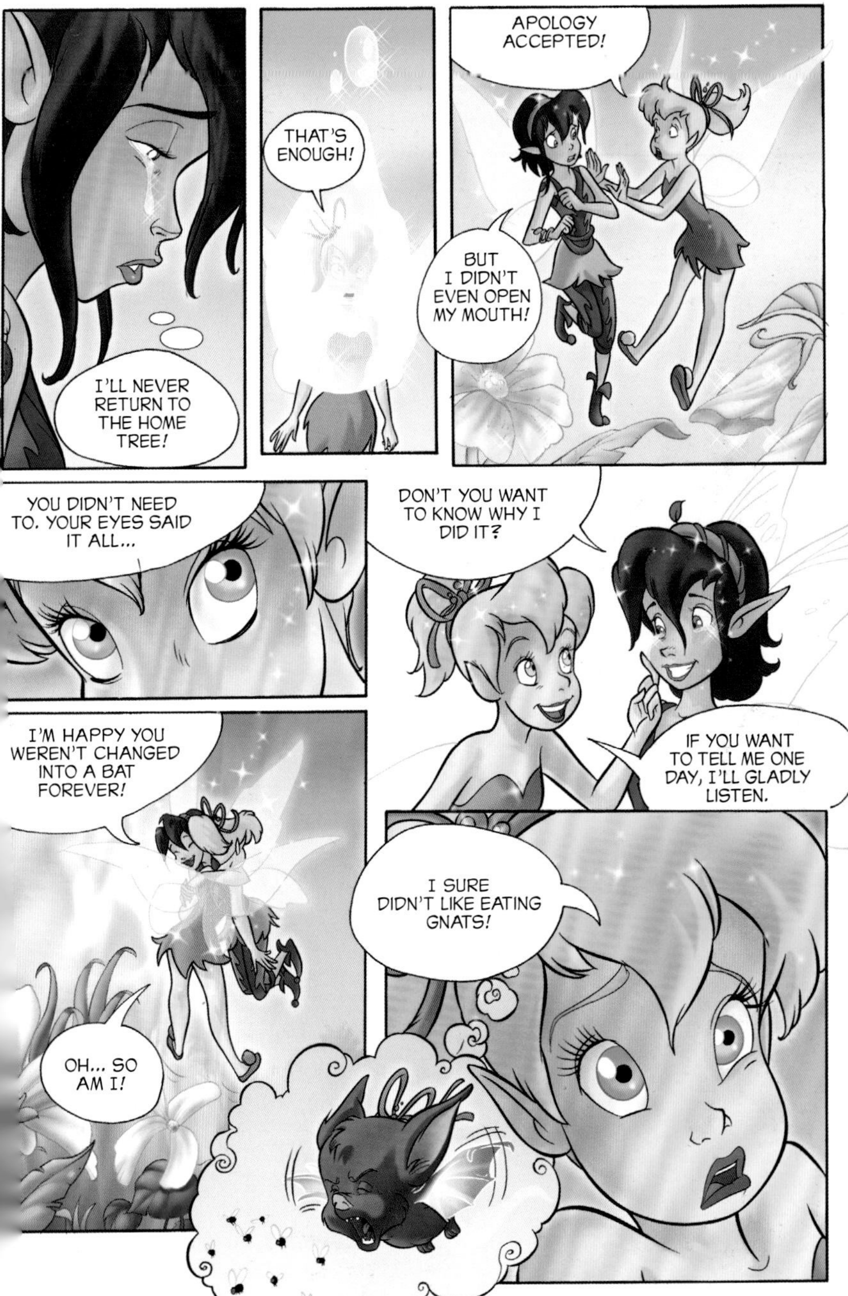

I'LL NEVER RETURN TO THE HOME TREE!
THAT'S ENOUGH!
APOLOGY ACCEPTED!
BUT I DIDN'T EVEN OPEN MY MOUTH!
YOU DIDN'T NEED TO. YOUR EYES SAID IT ALL...
DON'T YOU WANT TO KNOW WHY I DID IT?
IF YOU WANT TO TELL ME ONE DAY, I'LL GLADLY LISTEN.
I'M HAPPY YOU WEREN'T CHANGED INTO A BAT FOREVER!
OH... SO AM I!
I SURE DIDN'T LIKE EATING GNATS!

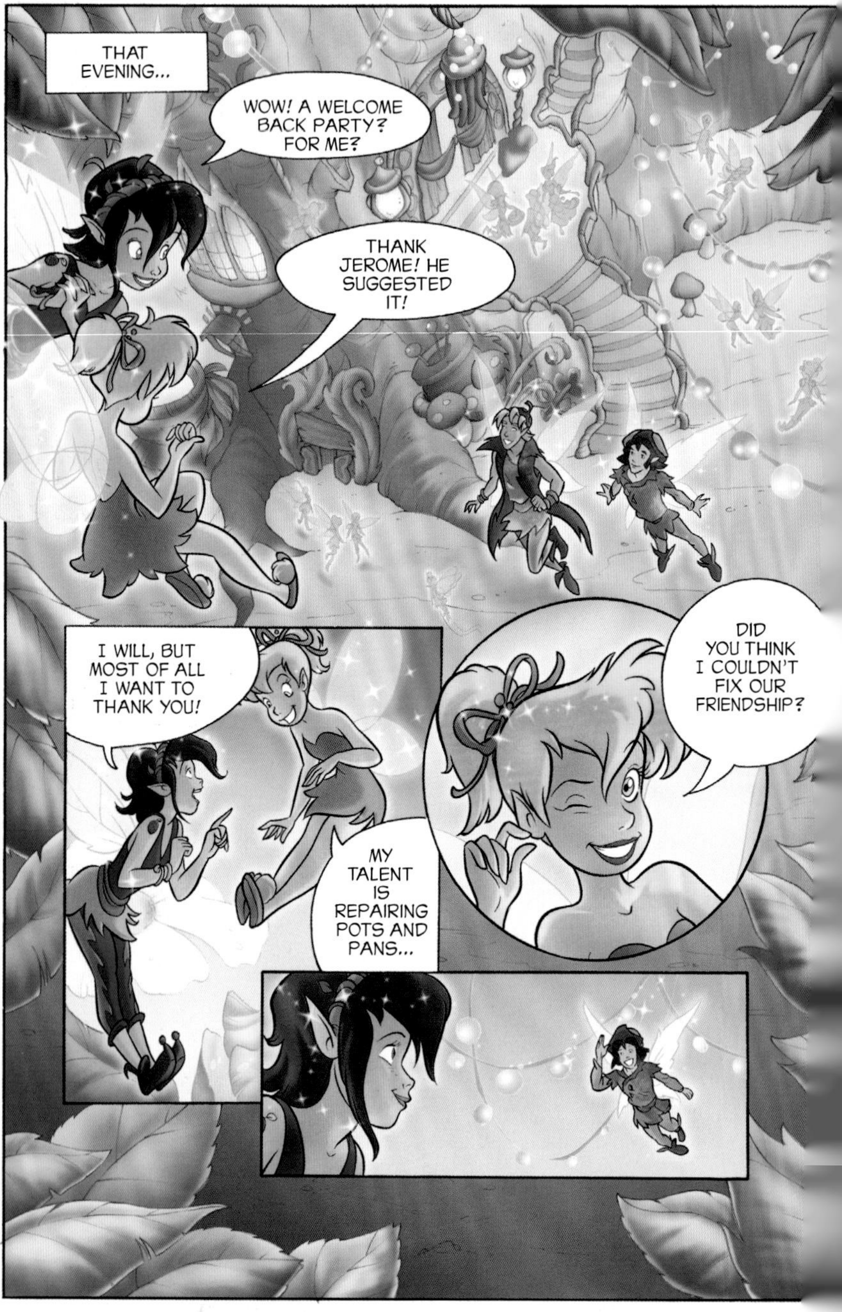
THAT EVENING...
WOW! A WELCOME BACK PARTY? FOR ME?
THANK JEROME! HE SUGGESTED IT!
I WILL, BUT MOST OF ALL I WANT TO THANK YOU!
MY TALENT IS REPAIRING POTS AND PANS...
DID YOU THINK I COULDN'T FIX OUR FRIENDSHIP?

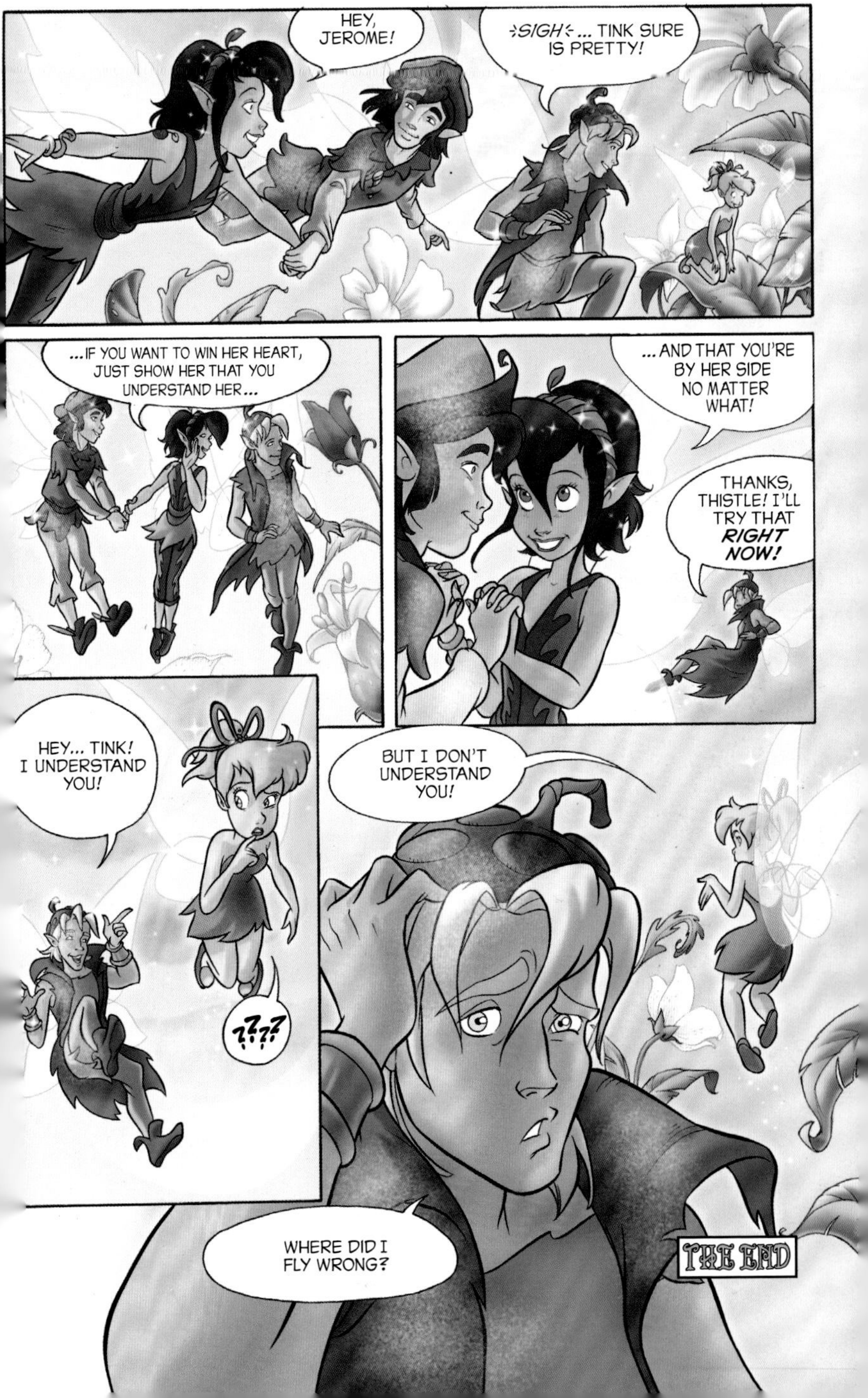
HEY, JEROME!
⊰SIGH⊱... TINK SURE IS PRETTY!
...IF YOU WANT TO WIN HER HEART, JUST SHOW HER THAT YOU UNDERSTAND HER...
...AND THAT YOU'RE BY HER SIDE NO MATTER WHAT!
THANKS, THISTLE! I'LL TRY THAT RIGHT NOW!
HEY... TINK! I UNDERSTAND YOU!
???
BUT I DON'T UNDERSTAND YOU!
WHERE DID I FLY WRONG?
THE END

WATCH OUT FOR PAPERCUTZ™

Welcome to the fourth fairy-dust covered DISNEY FAIRIES graphic novel from Papercutz. I'm Jim Salicrup, Editor-in-Chief and your Pixie Hollow tour guide. I'm here to let you in on all the new and exciting stuff going on at Papercutz. For example, we're publishing this wonderful series of graphic novels that feature these wonderful tiny characters that live in a magical land, in homes that couldn't possibly be more "green," as in environmentally-friendly. While one among them is their leader, living not that far away is one of their most fearsome foes! Can you guess the Papercutz series I'm talking about? Did you guess, DISNEY FAIRIES? They live in Never Land, in Pixie Hollow, in the Home Tree, ruled by Queen Clarion, and not that far away from mean ol' Captain Hook! That's a great guess, but it's not the graphic novel series I'm talking about.

Here's another clue—these wonderful tiny characters are all blue! (I guess you can call this a "Blue Clue.")

If you guessed THE SMURFS, you're 100% correct! They all live in the Smurf Village, in little homes carved out of large mushrooms, where Papa Smurf looks after them all, while the wicked sorcerer Gargamel lives not that far away!

On the following pages we offer a preview from SMURFS Graphic Novel #1"The Purple Smurfs." Check it out, it's smurf-tastic!

And just to remind you that the graphic novel version of TINKER BELL AND THE GREAT FAIRY RESCUE DVD is also still available from Papercutz, we offer an exclusive excerpt right after the SMURFS preview! Don't forget that the actual pages of the TINKER BELL AND THE GREAT FAIRIES RESCUE are larger than what appears here! And don't get your wings all twisted up if it's sold out at your favorite bookstore—you can still order it online or from us (see page 80).

In the meantime, let us know what you thought of this DISNEY FAIRIES graphic novel! We really liked how all the individual stories told an ever bigger story about Thistle and Tinker Bell. But what did you think? Would you like to see one big long story in DISNEY FAIRIES or do you like seeing lots of shorter stories? Send us your comments and we'll present some of the best ones in an upcoming DISNEY FAIRIES graphic novel. Either email your criticisms or praise or both to me at: Salicrup@papercutz.com or mail them to me at: DISNEY FAIRIES, Papercutz, 160 Broadway, Suite 700, East Wing, New York, NY 10038.

So until DISNEY FAIRIES #5 "Tinker Bell and the Pirate Adventure," remember "Faith, Trust, and Pixie Dust!"

JIM

STAY IN TOUCH!

EMAIL: salicrup@papercutz.com
WEB: www.papercutz.com
TWITTER: @papercutzgn
FACEBOOK: PAPERCUTZGRAPHICNOVELS
SNAIL MAIL: Papercutz, 160 Broadway
            Suite 700, East Wing
            New York, NY 10038

Special preview of the SMURFS™ Graphic Novel #1 "The Purple Smurfs"...

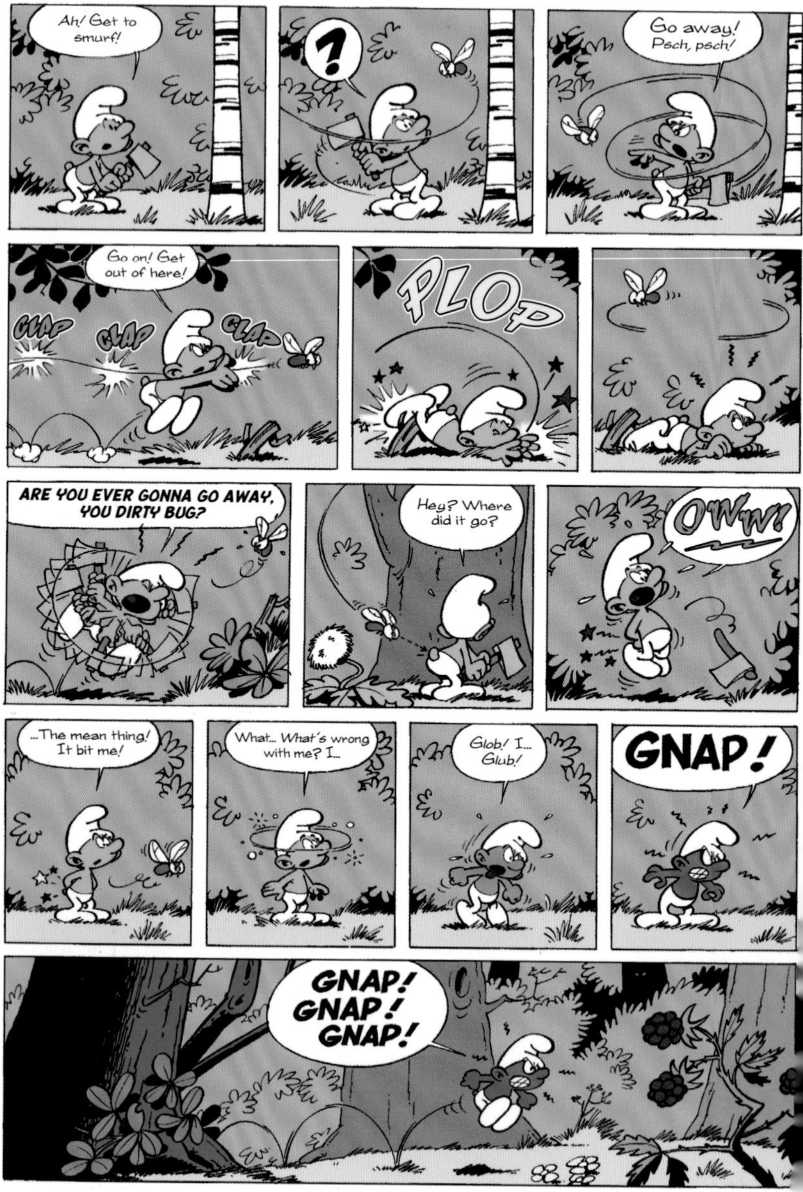
Ah! Get to smurf!
?
Go away! Psch, psch!
Go on! Get out of here!
CLAP
CLAP
CLAP
PLOP
ARE YOU EVER GONNA GO AWAY, YOU DIRTY BUG?
Hey? Where did it go?
OWW!
...The mean thing! It bit me!
What... What's wrong with me? I...
Glob! I... Glub!
GNAP!
GNAP! GNAP! GNAP!

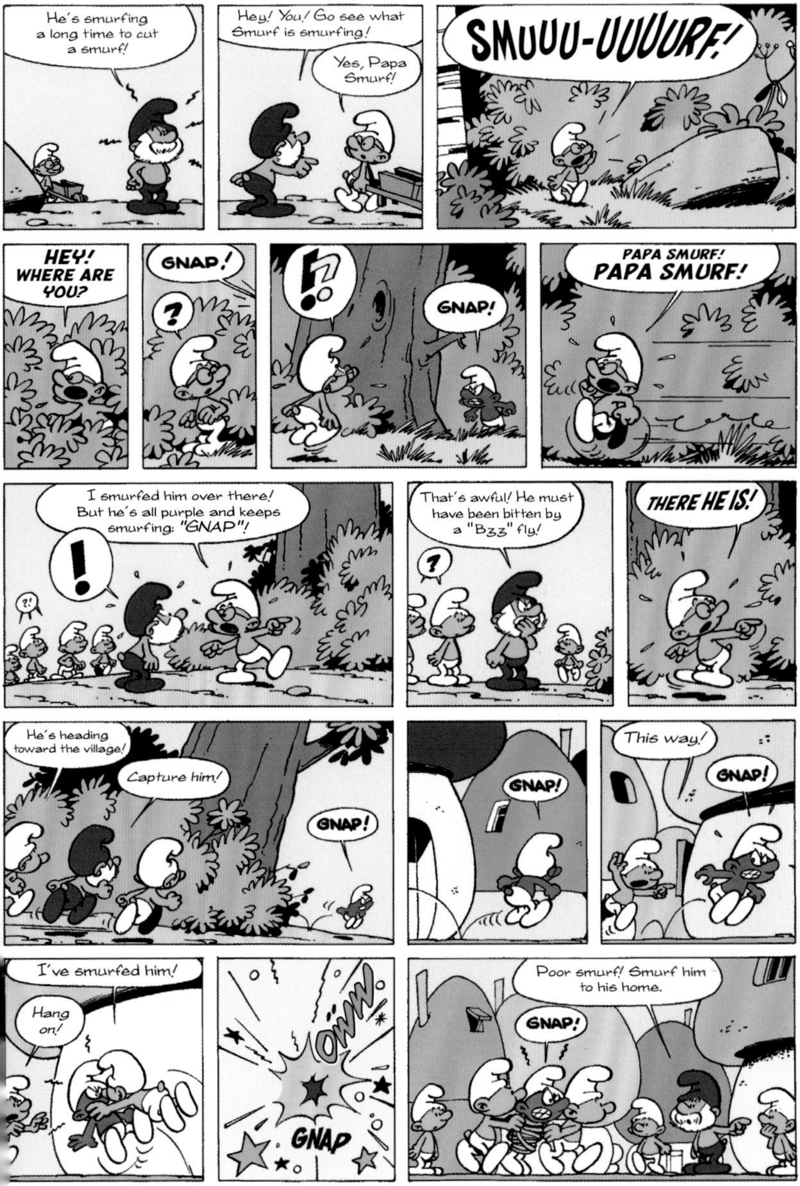
He's smurfing a long time to cut a smurf!
Hey! You! Go see what Smurf is smurfing!
Yes, Papa Smurf!
SMUUU-UUUURF!
HEY! WHERE ARE YOU?
GNAP!
?
!?
GNAP!
PAPA SMURF! PAPA SMURF!
I smurfed him over there! But he's all purple and keeps smurfing: "GNAP"!
!
?!
That's awful! He must have been bitten by a "Bzz" fly!
?
THERE HE IS!
He's heading toward the village!
Capture him!
GNAP!
GNAP!
This way!
GNAP!
I've smurfed him!
Hang on!
OWW
GNAP
Poor smurf! Smurf him to his home.
GNAP!

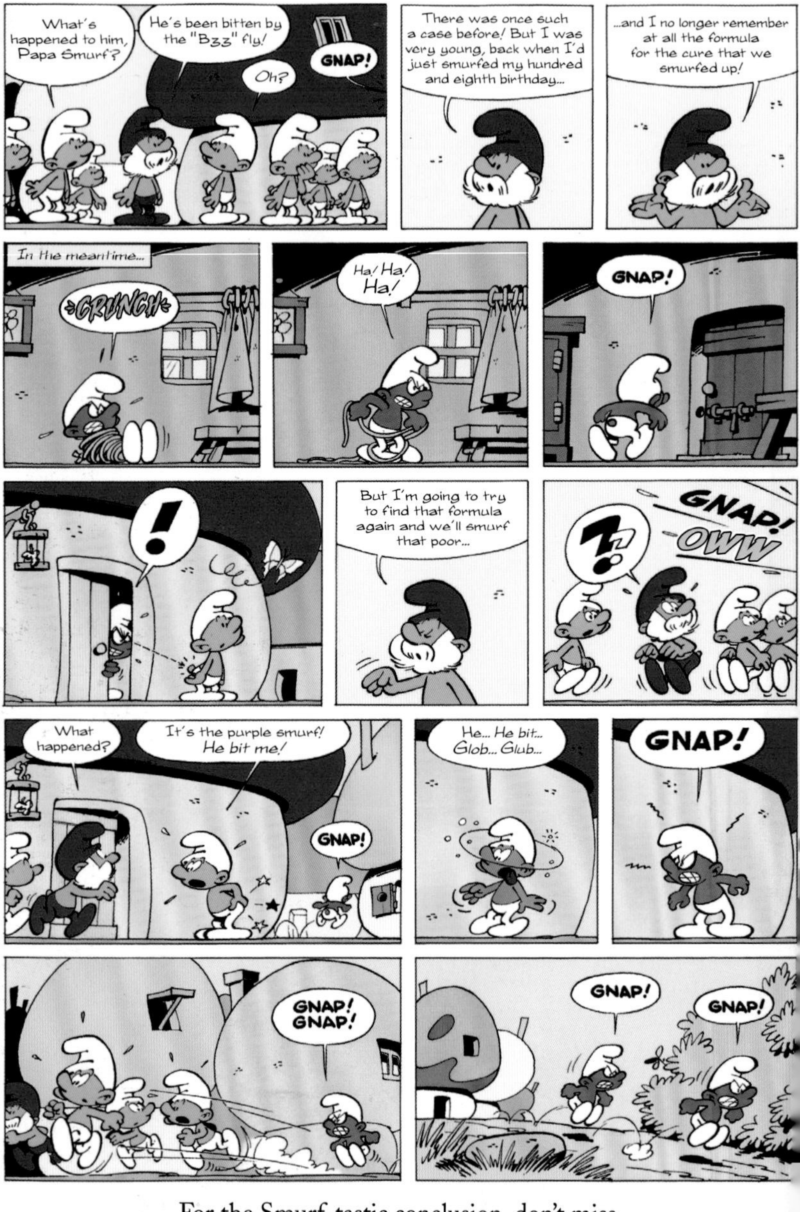
What's happened to him, Papa Smurf?
He's been bitten by the "Bzz" fly!
Oh?
GNAP!
There was once such a case before! But I was very young, back when I'd just smurfed my hundred and eighth birthday...
...and I no longer remember at all the formula for the cure that we smurfed up!
In the meantime...
CRUNCH
Ha! Ha! Ha!
GNAP!
!
But I'm going to try to find that formula again and we'll smurf that poor...
GNAP!
OWW
?
What happened?
It's the purple smurf! He bit me!
GNAP!
He... He bit... Glob... Glub...
GNAP!
GNAP! GNAP!
GNAP!
GNAP!

For the Smurf-tastic conclusion, don't miss

the SMURFS Graphic Novel #1 "The Purple Smurfs"!

the SMURFS™

GRAPHIC NOVELS AVAILABLE AT BOOKSELLERS EVERYWHERE AND WHEREVER DIGITAL BOOKS ARE SOLD.

PURPLE
SMURFS
Graphic Novel #1

THE SMURFS AND THE
MAGIC FLUTE
Graphic Novel #2

THE SMURF
KING
Graphic Novel #3

SMURFETTE
Graphic Novel #4

THE SMURFS AND THE
EGG
Graphic Novel #5

THE SMURFS AND THE
HOWLIBIRD
Graphic Novel #6

THE ASTRO
SMURF
Graphic Novel #7

THE SMURF
APPRENTICE
Graphic Novel #8

GARGAMEL
AND THE SMURFS
Graphic Novel #9

THE RETURN OF
SMURFETTE
Graphic Novel #10

THE SMURF
OLYMPICS
Graphic Novel #11

SMURF
VS.
SMURF
Graphic Novel #12

EACH GRAPHIC NOVEL IS 100% SMURFY!

SMURF™

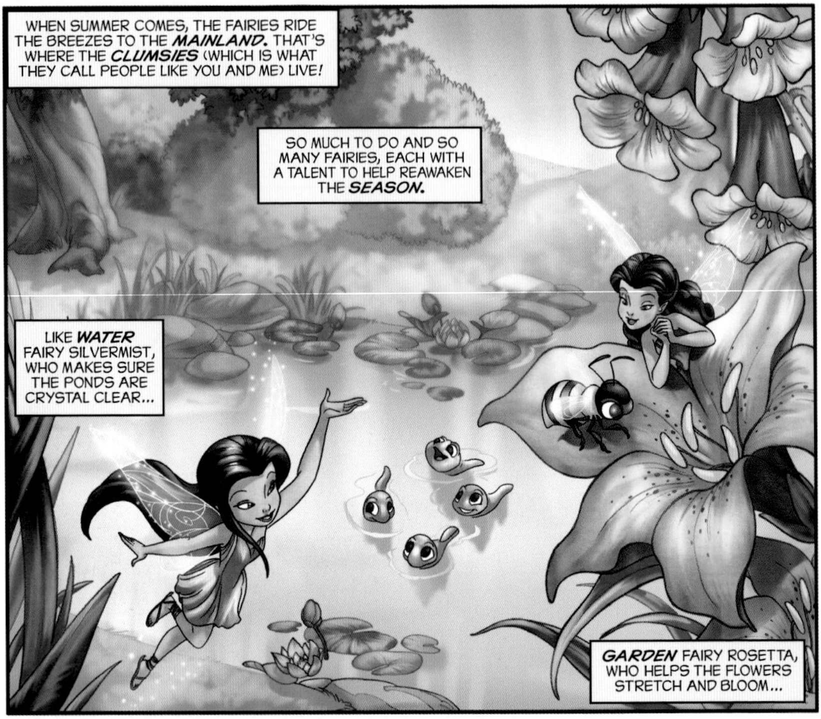
WHEN SUMMER COMES, THE FAIRIES RIDE THE BREEZES TO THE MAINLAND. THAT'S WHERE THE CLUMSIES (WHICH IS WHAT THEY CALL PEOPLE LIKE YOU AND ME) LIVE!
SO MUCH TO DO AND SO MANY FAIRIES, EACH WITH A TALENT TO HELP REAWAKEN THE SEASON.
LIKE WATER FAIRY SILVERMIST, WHO MAKES SURE THE PONDS ARE CRYSTAL CLEAR...
GARDEN FAIRY ROSETTA, WHO HELPS THE FLOWERS STRETCH AND BLOOM...

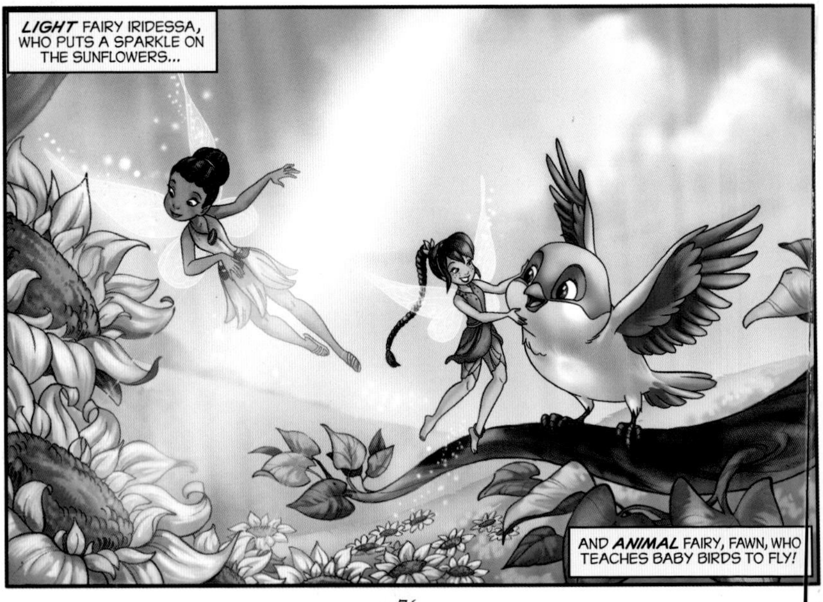
LIGHT FAIRY IRIDESSA, WHO PUTS A SPARKLE ON THE SUNFLOWERS...
AND ANIMAL FAIRY, FAWN, WHO TEACHES BABY BIRDS TO FLY!

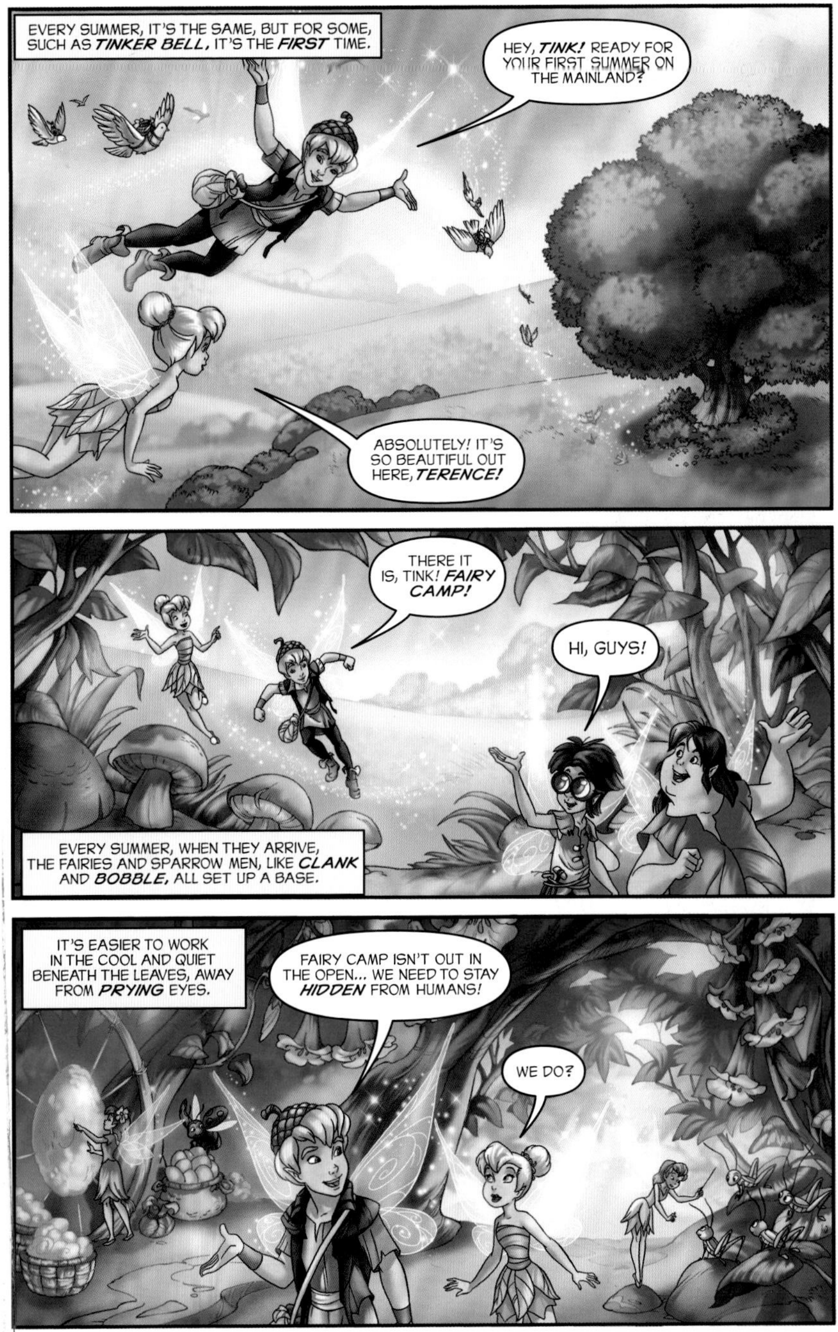
EVERY SUMMER, IT'S THE SAME, BUT FOR SOME, SUCH AS TINKER BELL, IT'S THE FIRST TIME.
HEY, TINK! READY FOR YOUR FIRST SUMMER ON THE MAINLAND?
ABSOLUTELY! IT'S SO BEAUTIFUL OUT HERE, TERENCE!
THERE IT IS, TINK! FAIRY CAMP!
HI, GUYS!
EVERY SUMMER, WHEN THEY ARRIVE, THE FAIRIES AND SPARROW MEN, LIKE CLANK AND BOBBLE, ALL SET UP A BASE.
IT'S EASIER TO WORK IN THE COOL AND QUIET BENEATH THE LEAVES, AWAY FROM PRYING EYES.
FAIRY CAMP ISN'T OUT IN THE OPEN... WE NEED TO STAY HIDDEN FROM HUMANS!
WE DO?

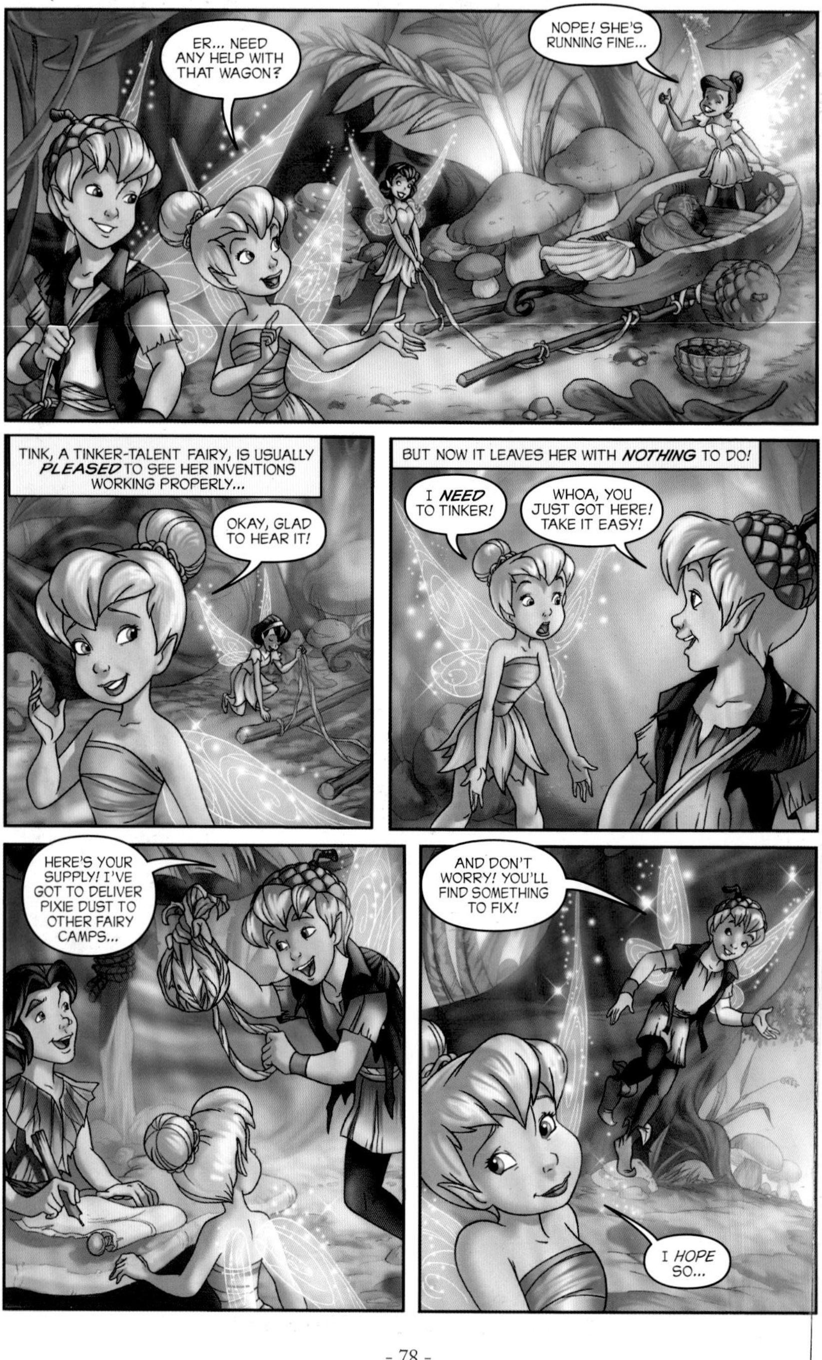
ER... NEED ANY HELP WITH THAT WAGON?
NOPE! SHE'S RUNNING FINE...
TINK, A TINKER-TALENT FAIRY, IS USUALLY PLEASED TO SEE HER INVENTIONS WORKING PROPERLY...
OKAY, GLAD TO HEAR IT!
BUT NOW IT LEAVES HER WITH NOTHING TO DO!
I NEED TO TINKER!
WHOA, YOU JUST GOT HERE! TAKE IT EASY!
HERE'S YOUR SUPPLY! I'VE GOT TO DELIVER PIXIE DUST TO OTHER FAIRY CAMPS...
AND DON'T WORRY! YOU'LL FIND SOMETHING TO FIX!
I HOPE SO...

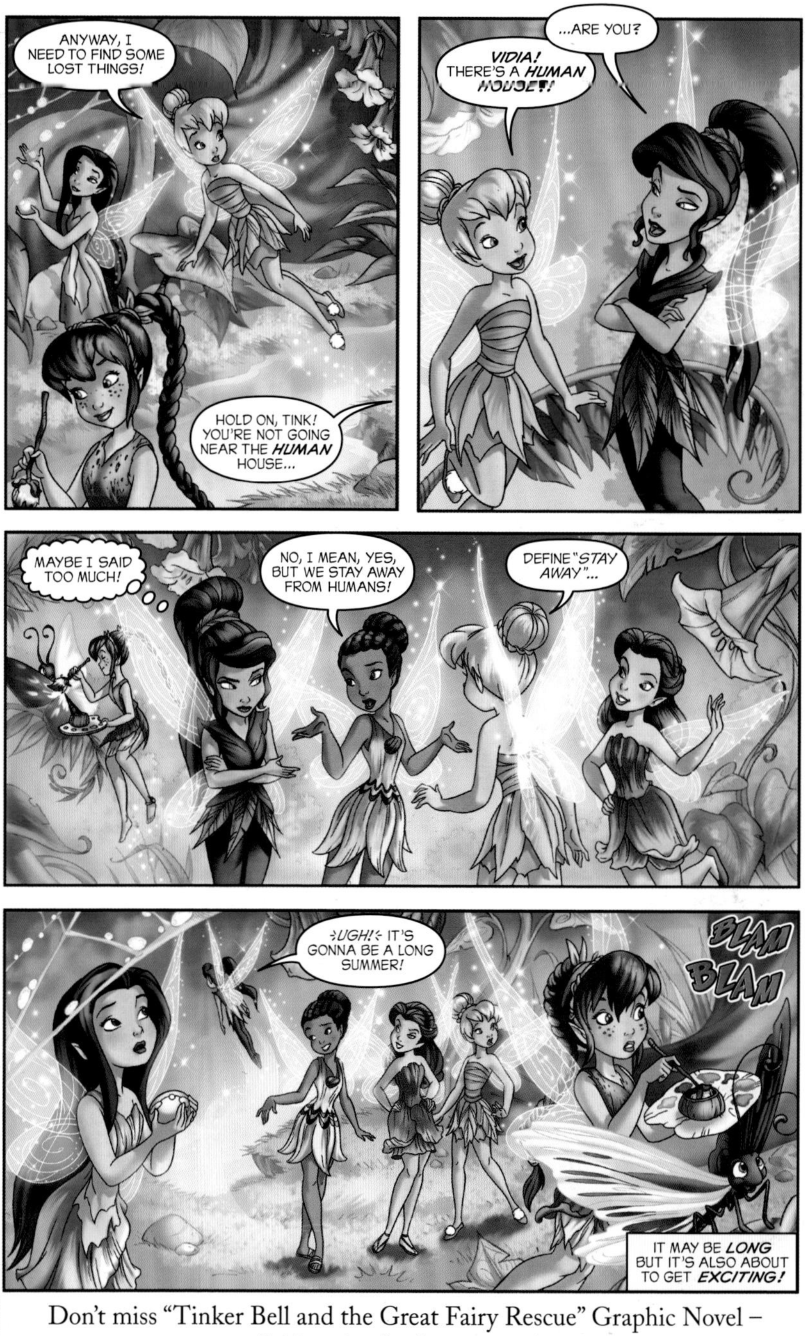
ANYWAY, I NEED TO FIND SOME LOST THINGS!
HOLD ON, TINK! YOU'RE NOT GOING NEAR THE *HUMAN* HOUSE...
VIDIA! THERE'S A *HUMAN HOUSE?!*
...ARE YOU?
MAYBE I SAID TOO MUCH!
NO, I MEAN, YES, BUT WE STAY AWAY FROM HUMANS!
DEFINE "*STAY AWAY*"...
UGH! IT'S GONNA BE A LONG SUMMER!
BLAM
BLAM
IT MAY BE ***LONG*** BUT IT'S ALSO ABOUT TO GET ***EXCITING!***

Don't miss "Tinker Bell and the Great Fairy Rescue" Graphic Novel – available at booksellers everywhere!